FROM THE LIBRARY OF

Kathy Martín

Also by CECILY CROWE

The Tower of Kilraven
Northwater

tHE
Twice-born

THE
TWICE-bORN

Cecily Crowe

Random House
New York

Library of Congress Cataloging in Publication Data
Crowe, Cecily.
   The twice-born.
   I. Title.
PZ4.C95298Tw   [PS3553.R59]   813'.5'4   72–1058
ISBN 0–394–47554–2
Manufactured in the United States of America by The Book Press
Brattleboro, Vt.
9 8 7 6 5 4 3 2
First Edition

for Midge

THE
Twice-born

1

An extraordinary thing happened to Faith Farrell when she was sixteen, a metamorphosis.

Scrawny, feverish, laughing too much in the adolescent way of braving the world, witlessly attracting attention to herself, miserably in love with one high-school hero after another who ignored her, failing in all grades, she was abruptly removed by her parents from the Beechwood school she had attended from childhood and sent to St. Anne's in Manhattan. She was sent to this Episcopalian day school not because her parents were in any way religious but because the school had a reputation for severity and high academic standing. Such Olympian transactions could take place incontestably over Faith's head; her father did, however, let fall the opinion that it was his own name that had persuaded Miss Calcott, the school's headmistress, to accept her, although her mother thought the respectful manners of

Faith's upbringing had something to do with it. "You are welcome," said Miss Calcott, looking Faith calmly in the eye, as if nothing, neither good manners nor an illustrious parent, could sway her against her better judgment, "as long as you are serious about your studies; otherwise you will be wasting your time and ours and you will be dismissed."

So from her suburban school of invidious cliques, giggling and crushes, where boring Latin or math were only incidental to the socio-sexual skirmish, Faith found herself secluded from boys in a churchly Gothic building, thrust among girls who were studious and mannerly by selection, tall city girls with a calm not unlike Miss Calcott's—an atmosphere at once civilized and cerebral. What Faith's parents didn't expect was that she would take to it like a duck to water. Despite the new school's formalities and restrictions (daily chapel, Bible studies, no high heels, no lipstick), it offered inexplicably a greater freedom than the harum-scarum Beechwood school, a respect Faith had never known in her own home, a cloistered worldliness in which she found a heady relief.

It was no surprise that her talent was recognized; she had always been the class artist, a distinction she had never considered as prestigious as being the class athlete or even the class mimic, and besides, she had grown up in a house where artistic excellence was taken for granted. She was duly elected to the art committee of St. Anne's yearbook staff, given charge of the sets for the junior-senior play, eventually invited to paint a permanent frieze around the walls of the art room, in which she drolly portrayed St. Anne's girls in Greek posture.

What was much more revolutionary and exhilarating was the encouragement to think, to dare to think for herself, an encouragement spearheaded in English III by Mrs. Bent-Ufford, a thin, gray, slightly hunchbacked woman, who with a sharp gray wit and a caustic sarcasm dredged up the imagination of her decorous pupils and forced them to express it intelligibly. It was no wonder St. Anne's was reputed to "rank highest in English of all Eastern schools," as St. A. girls were fond of stating.

"Now, come, Faith, don't look like a frightened doe. If you have read this passage with any degree of curiosity, you should be able to hazard a guess as to Ophelia's virginity. Or do you consider virginity irrelevant?" Titters, blushes, but no hard feelings. It was too exciting, being escalated to Mrs. Bent-Ufford's plane of somewhat cynical intelligence. (*Virginity*, like *sex* and *God*, was a word never uttered in Faith's home, where art, agnosticism and prudery were so perilously combined.) In Mrs. Bent-Ufford's room they sat not at desks but at two long tables facing the Gothic windows, as though facing the tall bleached light of erudition, while Mrs. Bent-Ufford roamed up and down before them, cajoling, staring out at the street, coughing a dreadful cigarette cough, grinning slyly.

Almost overnight Faith became a stately young woman.

She had been the most painful of wallflowers, an angular, self-conscious figure from whom everyone averted his eyes; but now the pointed chin softened, the wary fox-eyes steadied, widened and deepened in color, and the carroty hair, which in fact had been darkening over the years, became tractable and glossy, waved close to the head in the fashion of the day. Her sallow skin, rounding out, grew marbled, delicately responsive to mood and climate. An inevitable physical development, no doubt, but one that couldn't have come about with such overtones of allure in the old Beechwood milieu where the stigma of the outcast historically clung to her. At St. Anne's, all that had formerly made her "different"—her talent, her sensitivity, her inappropriate dreaminess and times of seeming withdrawn—all at once made her distinguished and rather mysterious.

Now, commuting on trains and subways, she was stared at covetously by grown men. The old high-school heroes encountered occasionally in Beechwood gave her an astonished, abashed double-take, as if betrayed, and soon she could afford to pick and choose among them, and sometimes, pleasurably, be cruel to them. With her air of removal to the sophistication of the city, she acquired in Beechwood the then-enviable reputation of being "high hat."

Her flowering coincided, luckily, with the new feminine ideal, successor to the peppy, jiggling girls of the twenties: a young woman not only of elegance and mystery and repose but of some inner melancholy. Times had changed, the stock market had crashed, and although the full impact of the Depression was yet to be felt, flippancy had come to an end: Clara Bow was succeeded by Greta Garbo. They wore black, these subdued young women of the early thirties, and pearls, their long legs simply shod in black suede pumps, and how proudly, how broodingly, as though already doomed, they stepped out of taxis and town cars, crossed the lobby of the Biltmore or the Pierre Restaurant on Park Avenue or the old Voisin's, rode the New Haven to Boston, took ship with their chaperones to Europe. By the time she was seventeen Faith Farrell, moving with a tender caution, head erect, cheeks slightly flushed, had begun to represent this prototype herself, tea-dancing at the St. Regis, driving to games at Yale or West Point, even stepping now and then from a town car—the elderly Rolls-Royce belonging to the family of Janice Pemberton, a St. Anne's classmate who invited Faith to the opera on Monday nights.

Not that she had become wildly popular. (In her yearbook she was not voted Most Popular or Most Beautiful, but the girl with the Biggest Future.) She was still too anomalous, too intrinsically shy, and her self-threatening anxiety still made itself known, her moments of warmth and ease and humor giving way to a woodenness as stony as rejection, an embarrassing embarrassment. There was often something ghostly about her; it showed in her face, as if left to herself she had little substance or sense of self.

"But of course I didn't outgrow that contemptible childhood overnight," she told Dr. Pomeroy, years later when her private doom had come at last to hover over her. "The unloved and unlovable and unloving child still groped around in there."

Sometimes Dr. Pomeroy's broad-viewing eyes sharpened briefly on her in an amused focus.

"Maybe being a swan all of a sudden," she continued, "was even more fraught with danger than being loathsome."

"Faith, you were not loathsome."

"I was! Cringing, ravenous, ungainly—no wonder my father despised me. If I could see myself now as I was then, I would despise me."

"You despised yourself, then."

"Yes." Voicing truths with Dr. Pomeroy often brought an insoluble lump to her throat, silencing her.

In fact, Faith's metamorphosis was something of an affront to her parents. It was only natural that it should be so; cringing minors unknowingly make themselves useful. Her parents needed her as a repository for their difficulties between themselves, and from early childhood Faith sensed that the role she was expected to play was unlovely.

"Oh God, Faith, don't *skulk!*" her father would roar, meeting her in the hall as he emerged naked from the bathroom, holding his robe in front of him, freshly showered, his red beard shining and all the little red hairs on his body moist and glistening. His stormy success was founded on uncompromising aesthetics, and he did not have the emotional make-up to tolerate the timid or less than beautiful. Yet with the odious word he held up to shame the very thing he knew (and knew that she knew) she must do in his presence. It was one of those bizarre and sinister family games, unsuspected by outsiders.

And in the background, with darting, bulging dark eyes, Faith's mother kept watch on her for the slightest sign of defiance or disrespect, the left hand with the wedding ring ever ready to fly out across Faith's mouth, the ring bruising the lips. Were they, for some unfathomable reason, jealous of her?

In time the only child became the only tie between Jack Farrell's increasing fame and embrace of the "smart" world of the city, and Clara Farrell's retreat into homely domesticity, her increasing recourse to "plainness," a kind of old-fashioned, dowdy, anti-sexual, even anti-feminine, virtue. Only with Faith—a mutual cross to bear, like a mutual antagonist—could this divergent couple live together with some degree of accord. And then Faith's swan-change took place, shaking the ground under their feet.

Her mother's awful glares ceased, the hand no longer slapped. She turned her face away from Faith's beauty as if it implied indecency, a final insult, and took refuge in renouncing silences, becoming ever plainer, more immobile, more neuter in brown tweeds, an object of defeat. She lost interest in housework, once a violent demonstration of virtue, abandoning it to the maid they could now afford, and withdrew to the big front bedroom she and Jack had shared before he moved to the guest room. Now she kept a card table set up for solitaire and crossword puzzles; and there Faith came home to find her day after day, huddled in a chair in front of the leaded windows, the curtains never drawn even after dark, as if she were indifferent to the eyes of the world itself. When Faith greeted her, she answered reproachfully with a throat-sound rather than a word, not looking up.

"She was deeply depressed—wasn't she?—and I had no comprehension of it or compassion. I was congenitally obtuse, a congenital egotist."

And Dr. Pomeroy, biased, of course, in her favor, answered, "And how did you get to be that way?"

She gave him a stubborn lump of a look, as if to say *Don't*. She had always felt guilt for her mother's destiny, and she couldn't add to it the guilt of blaming her mother for her own destiny. "But maybe I exaggerate them! Maybe they weren't like that at all. I leave out everything good about them, my father's brilliance, my mother's humor, her—*strength*. I'm not giving you a true picture of them!"

"It doesn't matter," he told her. "The important thing is, this is the way you felt about them."

Her mother became an accusation she couldn't contest, a problem she couldn't solve, an uneasy, sorrowing responsibility she didn't know how to accept. When she went out in the evening with a beau, her mother responded to her goodnight with a glum "Don't be late." Her morosity went down the stairs and out the door with Faith like an evil spell, encasing her and weighing on her, and she got into the young man's car with a sigh and found it hard to be sociable until they had left Beechwood behind. Later in the evening the discomfort would begin to unsettle her again and compel her homeward.

She felt doubly guilty because she couldn't help comparing her mother with May Morrison, who was her father's cousin and lived directly across the street in one of the little pseudo-Tudor row houses. Faith had grown up with May's children, Pamela and Jeff, and theirs was a household she adored, was always welcome in, felt snug in. On rainy afternoons in their early years May would light the gas logs in the tiny sitting room and say, "Now you children curl up here in front of the fire and read," and this they would do, as quiet as mice. And when Pamela and Faith set out together, to dancing school or a birthday party, and later to more grown-up affairs, there was May, blond and freckled, seeing them off, breathing her blond laugh over them: "Have a good time, girls! Have a lovely time!" And unbeautiful or not, they went off feeling like girls, like girls having a lovely time!

Her father's reaction to her blossoming was even more drastic. The more desirable Faith was to others, the more obsessed he became with retaining his authority over her; the more stately her appearance, the more degrading his commands—ruling on her lipstick, her cigarettes, the tidiness of her room, the hour of her return from an evening's engagement. He would stalk outdoors at midnight in his bathrobe and order her out of a car where she was having an innocent goodnight chat. In his presence she now broke out in a nervous perspiration, which he pounced on, too, commenting on it publicly and aggravating the condition.

There were also the times when he was meltingly indulgent, bringing tears to his own eyes, for he was easily moved by sentiment: when he bestowed his permission or granted her wishes beneficently, when he invited her and a comely classmate to lunch at Voisin's, one of his haunts, or arranged a grand catered dinner party for her in his office in New York, which was adaptable to entertaining. But often she would discover his eyes resting on her as though feasting, not unlike the eyes of men on subways and trains, and the full moist lips framed in the red beard wore a little triumphant smile. And these moments were more unnerving than his fury.

There was only one area where they could meet without danger, and this was the realm of art. Although he worked in architecture, he was thoroughly knowledgeable in other fields, his interest a steadfast passion, and he sponsored Faith's painting with a magnanimous hands-off partisanship. (In fact, he was generous with all young artists who came to him for advice, and freely gave them of his time and experience and, most importantly, his serious respect.) He had always encouraged Faith, bringing home for her, along with his own blueprints, the most enticing blocks of paper, the most tempting pens and pencils and inks, all exquisitely wrapped by Miss Hovis, his secretary. He provided her with sable brushes, Winsor & Newton colors, German chalks, the finest canvas, art books and magazines printed in foreign languages: everything well made and equally well cared for, so that with these impeccable packages he brought her, too, an acquaintance with a world of excellence, of order and clean-lined design and function, a kind of incorruptible truth in itself. "Darling, never make do with anything second-rate." He could call her *darling* when they met on this purified plateau.

Now that she was in her teens, he dispatched her with her mother to view a rare exhibit of Impressionists in Chicago, or a new collection in Philadelphia, sent them abroad primarily to see Chartres. He set her an example of open-mindedness to the new and experimental, for in his own field he was a pioneer. And for all that he was a man who could no more help imposing his will than he could help having red hair, he never told her how to paint.

She developed an irrevocable ambivalence toward him. When their minds met in the pure atmosphere of art, it was the inviolate best of himself he gave her and it became the inviolate best of herself. But his humiliations ("Faith's got B.O. again!"), his petty tyrannies ("Come back upstairs and shut your closet door!"), his savage ridicule of her young men, aroused in her a hatred so unbounded, so help-less, that it could only be endured as despair: a despair of hatred that made herself its victim. Frequently in these years of her flowering she suffered moments of utter de-spondency, shutting herself in her room and lying face down on her bed and giving herself up to a lonely unanswer-able anguish.

Yet in this same period she could feel heaped with blessings, and walking home from the Beechwood station on winter evenings, she wanted to sing, or cry, for joy.

Emmet Drake, one of the old high-school heroes, was in love with her, as well as Bob Walls, a neophyte banker, rather self-important, whom she had met through her St. Anne's classmates; and *she* was in love with Tony Pember-ton, Princetonian, older brother of Janice, whose parents owned the respectable Rolls—blue-eyed, sandy-haired, "smooth," flirting with her winningly and just a little pa-tronizingly (she was after all only a high-school girl), and never asking her for a date. A voluptuous misery, to be hopelessly in love!

She walked differently then, and a potent energy warmed her veins, and there seemed to be nothing she couldn't give or receive or understand. She felt greater than herself, and although she knew her mother would disapprove of such self-aggrandizement, twitching her lids and turning her face away, Faith in this liberated mood felt entirely free of the guilt her mother exacted from her, just as at other times this rootless guilt canceled her. She even felt benevolent toward the boring, overly tended suburb, and under the velvet weight of dusk, with its delicate trees and the warm apricot lights glowing within its houses, it had never seemed cozier, safer or lovelier. A grace domed its crisp sky, and shining secrets were abroad for anyone to guess at, and she was in love, she was loved.

Thus everything in her life seemed two-sided: outer beauty shackled with an old inner unloveliness, love coupled with hate, despair offsetting ecstasy. Long afterward she voiced the opinion that it was then, in her sixteenth or seventeenth year, that she must have ripened for the seed of danger, the fateful fusion of all her antitheses, the bearing of poisoned fruit.

It was Thanksgiving Day.

Clara Farrell roused from her apathy and banged and thumped and clamored in the old way all morning in the kitchen with Freda, the maid. Aromas of turkey and oysters and almonds boiled in olive oil permeated the house, as powerful in their way as the bangs and thumps, emanations of Clara's sudden fervor. The swinging door with its inset Chinese scroll groaned continuously between the dining room and pantry; extra leaves had been inserted in the table, and Faith, expected to appear useful although permitted to do little, had helped to lay the cloth her father had brought from Paris, exquisitely embroidered in the style commonly called "modernistic" (a word Jack abominated), and had set the table with the good silver. Freda had polished the cocktail shaker and matching cups, and Jack had prepared cocktails of gin—which came mysteriously from nowhere in these Prohibition days—and orange juice.

Then everything was ready and Jack scrutinized Faith and told her, "You may go upstairs and put some lipstick on," and even Clara changed her dress and dusted her nose unskillfully with powder. On the dot of one, Aunt Grace and Uncle Severance arrived in their grand car from New Jersey, and at once the house was filled with greetings and cries and shouts of laughter.

Most of the time Severance Keyes, Grace's husband, wore a protective veil of abstraction, a nervous, weary aloofness, just as he had once worn, ineradicably in Faith's memory, a white mask, glaring pitilessly at her over it, waiting for her to succumb to the unspeakable, suffocating cone which a nurse pressed over her face. For a long time after this ordeal, a tonsillectomy, she shrank from his ice-cold gray eyes, and she could never speak to him naturally because anything she said to him had a way of bouncing back as inane, an invasion of his intense, cold privacy. He could relax, apparently, only in music, particularly the opera, and in spurts of buffoonery, roaring at his own atrocious puns and practical jokes, behavior which Faith found doubly dismaying in a man usually so austere.

His wife, little Grace, Clara's younger sister, buffered him from the world, indulged his clowning, and with her placid fortitude, got between him and pestering patients. When he made an outrageous remark, was rudely deaf to an idle query, abruptly left the table to telephone the hospital, Grace made a soft little hoarse titter that somehow explained everything and soothed everyone's feelings, and only occasionally called him to task with a gentle firmness. Clara often referred to the childhood glory of Grace's hair

("She had long chestnut curls, and everyone made a pet of her"). Now it had turned gray, but she was still pretty and small, dressed neatly in blue or lavender or pink, rather like a plump little dove, and she had a calm, hoarse, nasal voice that filled Faith with peace and love.

Then one summer day in New England, where they were all vacationing, Faith, sixteen, and her uncle, waiting in separate cars parked side by side, while the sisters, Clara and Grace, explored an antique shop, began making up poetry together through their open car windows, a long, solemn narrative beginning: "This is the ballad of Frederic Staples/Born beneath New Hampshire maples ..." And as they completed each couplet Severance threw back his head and shouted for joy, and Faith was never again afraid of him and always afterward could make him laugh as a kindness to him.

His gray eyes seemed to her no longer icy, but sad, and although she couldn't then have put it into words, she knew his apparent coldness was his torment: the burden of his work, his loathing of it and his obsessive compensatory concern for his patients. Like an unhappy priest who has chosen the wrong vocation and finds himself saddled with responsibility for the slippery human soul, Severance was a mystic forced to deal with bodies—layers of fat, orifices, bloody entrails; he might have made a happier priest. His romantic nature was encased as if in armor in the metallic techniques of surgery, and his burden was his deep constraint and doubt, his guilt that he could not love enough or ennoble the sordid human organisms entrusted to him. And yet it was probably his disillusioned humanity that gave greatness to his work, a public success won from private failure.

Again it wasn't until Faith came to Dr. Pomeroy that her feelings for her uncle came welling up, filling her eyes with tears: she worshipped him. She adored and condoned and worshipped him. If there had been a sexual component in her girlhood regard for him, she was far too chaste and naïve to recognize it, and it was too much stilled by pity. She loved him, and little Aunt Grace, more deeply and trustingly and consistently than her own parents, or any other adults.

He was gazing at her now, across the living room, with sorrowing eyes, and this time he said gravely, almost accusingly, silencing everyone, as his impulsive remarks were apt to do, "You're older, Faith. You're much older."

She didn't know how to answer him; she could only lift her chin and smile, glancing sideways self-consciously. She was wearing a black velvet dress, collared and cuffed with white fur, and of course she did look more grown-up than the last time he had seen her, in summer.

But inwardly she felt a bottomless sinking, a desolation like that of a mother for a defective child. Could he see it, she asked herself, did it show in her face, what had happened since he had last seen her: the unbearable times of despair, when she had lain on her bed, face down, lost in wordless loneliness, and pressed her clasped hands as if in prayer against the hard wedge of her body which seemed to be the site of her loneliness? The first time it happened— the yearning explosion of herself—it had been an awesome discovery, sucking into its vacuum all feeling but amazement, far more awesome than any external and equally inexplicable phenomena such as gravity or electricity or an inevitable chemical reaction. Yet it was a fact of life, she was certain, simple and incontrovertible, however overpowering, almost an affectionate fact of life, as if it had been waiting for her all along, to be known by her, to console her, part of herself, a buried grandeur like her own heartbeat.

Fearfully she had caused it to happen again, since then, although not often, but always in moments of desolation. And always something vaster, more grieving than mere loneliness, flooded in to fill the aftermath, a sorrowing shame, a wilderness, opening another bleak view into a threatening void. She rose dislocated, full of fragmented pretense, cloaking herself automatically in optimism.

Severance then said, "Clara, you must have Faith photographed now, right now, before she gets any older." And Clara, with a quick frown, lowered her lids and made a small disclaiming sound.

But now, fortunately, the Morrisons arrived from across the street and everyone rose and crowded about them, May's fluttering voice rising to hover like a bird over the confusion of greetings. She had a deprecating way of moaning, sighing, softly laughing, setting everyone else to cooing too, and at once rendering the atmosphere light-hearted. George, her husband, kept in the background, yet participated with a silent offering of kindness and stability; everyone knew he was there and counted on him, for while May was buoyant, George was fundamental, a necessary balance.

Pamela, tall for fifteen, with a crown of golden hair like her mother's, took her place beside Faith on the piano bench, facing the room, where they could exchange asides while politely being party to the gathering. Jeff, Pamela's brother, would be along later. Always a moody, dignified lad, he had begun now that he was at college to hold himself aloof from sentimental family gatherings.

Everyone talked at once, and Jack rattled the cocktail shaker.

It was only in recent years that the Morrisons and Farrells had taken to observing special occasions with cocktails. May Morrison had started it, for she was the one who initiated anything daring, and it was proof of her charm that she could persuade Clara Farrell to join in, for Clara had not only an innate distrust of carefreeness but a more specific horror of drunkenness, because of her wayward father. ("Your grandfather *drank*," she told Faith, and sealed her lips sternly.) In fact, May Morrison had a good effect on the strait-laced woman, drawing out Clara's dry humor, encouraging her to "have fun," demonstrating that one could be gay and even naughtily lawbreaking and still be a perfect lady.

Clara sat near the door, ready to leave for the kitchen if she was needed, smiling, flushed, at ease. She wore an unbecoming print dress (the one "good" dress she allowed herself), its front lightly dusted with face powder, but amusement relaxed her dark, heavy-lidded eyes and she looked younger, fey and unpredictable, as she had looked in the photographs Jack had taken of her in the early days of their marriage; she looked like the girl who could toss off sprightly water colors, or satirical sketches of maidens in huge tam-o'-shanters, schoolmasters and disreputable cats. She was the woman everyone wished her to be and knew she was. And Jack, approaching her first with the brimming silver goblets, said with deepest respect and affection, "For you, my dear."

He was in his element, dispensing hospitality, face flushed, shoulders squared, his great chest swelling under a mustard-colored vest. "Try some of my medicine, Severance. No, not poison, dear fellow, how sardonic you are. It's a homeopathic concoction, the layman's panacea."

Faith watched her parents with her eyes widened, the corners of her lips turned up, appreciating them as if she scarcely knew them. Now they seemed incapable of perpetrating sly indignities; malevolence had vanished from the air as if it had never existed.

18

And arriving before her with the tray, her father, carried away by good will, said, "I think you could have one, too, Faith. You're seventeen now."

Clara protested faintly, "Oh, Jack!" but everyone else made festive sounds of approval, and Faith, coloring, knowing she had been promoted to a station of adulthood, put out her hand for the cold moist goblet.

Pamela, beside her, who from childhood had been spirited and irrepressible in an enviably collected way, cried, "Well, if Faith can have one, I can, too, can't I, Mother?"

"Oh, Pamela, I don't know," warbled May, becomingly deterring to their host, although her jolly indulgent face belied her uncertainty. For though Pamela was only fifteen, their relationship was almost sisterly in its easy confidence; they held nothing back from each other. "What do *you* think, Jack?"

"Why not?" he exclaimed. They must all be as one today; no one must be excluded from his gallantry. "It's Thanksgiving! Of course she can!"

Again everyone murmured approval, everyone was caught up in his mood, and only Clara sighed quaintly, wistfully, "Oh dear," in much the same way that mothers weep at their daughters' weddings, and everyone gently laughed.

Faith, waiting while the rest of the company was served, studied the orange liquid in the sweating silver goblet, and again she felt divided with contrary feelings. Until now she had never drunk anything containing alcohol, for she had absorbed some of her mother's phobia. On football weekends and house parties there was always an inexperienced girl who drank too much and spent the evening vomiting in the ladies' room, or a youth, damp and ashen of face, who passed out, and these spectacles revolted Faith and frightened her. In any case, it was socially acceptable

19

as well as medically advisable to refuse the dubious bootleg liquor of the day.

On the other hand, this was the elixir that seemed to signal her father's good will, to counteract her mother's melancholy, to represent all that was delightful and harmless in May Morrison. It made them giggle in anticipation before they had taken even the first sip, and giggle more afterward.

The orange liquid was strangely opaque, neither clear like gin nor vivid like orange juice, and in its cloudy mystery, like a Renaissance potion, it seemed to Faith to possess subtle powers of adaptability, as if its alchemy already applied to her—to her shyness, her fearfulness, her confusions, her tendency to optimism and flights of fancy, her love-proneness, even her shame—and was prepared to render something of all these complexities, change her as it did her elders, produce a Faith she herself didn't know.

"Look, everybody!" declared Pamela. "I'm a woman of the world!" She had lit a cigarette, which Faith didn't quite have the nerve to do, and she arched her brows and lowered her lids and held her cocktail at arm's length in a blasé pose, and there was another ripple of laughter. For the thousandth time Faith envied her. If only she could be as daring!

Everyone was served, and Jack took up a position with his back to the hearth and raised his goblet, and there was an expectant hush. "Let us give thanks," he proclaimed solemnly, and at once tears filled his eyes. He was not giving thanks to God, to be sure, but his words and his voice had sounded so inadvertently close to it that he had shaken himself into unwonted reverence. "Let us give thanks for the feast we are about to share, for the shelter of this beautiful house—if I do say so myself" (muted laughter; he had, of course, designed it), "for our good health. Above all, let us give thanks that we are together, a family, a family of friends, a family bound together in love and admiration."

He meant it, he believed it, and Faith in her own admiring indulgence would go along with it, although a distant part of her brain commented brazenly, as if Pamela had uttered it: *Says you.* She suppressed a giggle; yes, she too felt giggly, even before the first sip.

And then, following a general murmur of assent, everyone drank.

Nothing happened; nothing at all. Faith had expected the first swallow to produce something, perhaps another kind of explosion, and it did nothing. It tasted bitter, like medicine, infinitely disappointing.

"Oh, Jack," May crooned, "you do make a delicious cocktail!"

"*I* don't think it's so hot," Pamela muttered to Faith. "Do you?"

"No. *Bleagh.* Do I have to finish it?"

"Well, you can't pour it in the piano. I'm going to hold mine. I want to see Jeff's face when he comes in and sees me. Listen, let's pretend we're getting tight."

"Oh, no, Pam, *don't*," Faith cried, alarmed. "Please don't!"

"Okay, okay. Anyway, Mother's let me have a sip of her drink lots of times."

Faith turned to her in astonishment. Why hadn't Pam told her this before? But it was typical of the way Pamela and her mother minimized occasions and treats that in her own house would have loomed with consequence. There was always a half-eaten box of candy lying about the Morrisons' house ("It will *ruin* their teeth," said Clara), they had ice cream whenever they felt like it, or pancakes, and lobster in season and watermelon, delicacies Clara considered vaguely reprehensible. If Clara had ever allowed Faith a sip of her drink, Faith would have rushed across the street to tell Pam about it, but for Pam, it wasn't worth mentioning.

Everyone was chatting amiably when Jeff came in, trying to slip into the room inconspicuously. Conversations broke off and he was met with a chorus of greetings. Severance couldn't resist joshing him as he had done when Jeff was a stiff-spined boy, which made Jeff as usual flush angrily. But Jack, ceremoniously putting aside a long-standing antipathy (he was in fact jealous of all young men), pressed a cocktail on him, and there was a reshuffle of feet and chairs, and then Jeff chose to sit in a corner on the floor.

He was a good student, not so much brilliant as diligent, and he was at Williams on a scholarship, but lately his proud, tight-lipped, somewhat crooked face had grown haggard and secretive. His family adored him, especially May, and perhaps their sacrifices on his behalf, now that they were feeling the Depression, concerned and humiliated him, and he was working too hard. Recently he had mentioned getting through college in three years rather than four. A promising future was predicted for him.

Not by any stretch of the imagination could Faith have fallen in love with Jeff, although she felt for him an unexplained compassion. From childhood he had merely tolerated her, their cousinly relationship a formality, and even toward Pamela he had a supervisory air. When he brought friends home from college and they took the girls off in his Model T to the German-American Athletic Club in the Village, it was only after quite a lot of beer that anyone could get a laugh out of him.

Yet Jeff could be counted on to keep a promise, speak the truth, lend a helping hand. He was like his father, without his father's gentle twinkle. His lonely tension made itself felt, and while he aroused respect, he was also a little intimidating.

May broke the silence that had settled, exclaiming with a fluttering sigh, "Oh my, I'd rather be here with the Farrells and Keyeses than anyone else on earth. I feel positively euphoric."

"I think, my dear," said Jack, approaching her again with the cocktail shaker, "you are being euphemistic."

"No, Jack, the kind of euphoria I feel needs no euphemism."

"Euphoria or against her, Jack?" asked Severance, and broke into immense guffaws.

May and Jack commenced one of their verbal rallies, actually like a tennis rally, with everyone's head turning from one to the other, and the appreciative chuckles grew in volume, for their absurd banter, full of word play and double meanings, interspersed with Severance's foolery, was a highpoint of these gatherings.

And Faith listened with her eyes as well as her ears, taking in the scene like a spectator, a stranger, imagining how Tony Pemberton, for instance, the cavalier Princetonian whom she idolized, might see and hear and admire it: the wan November light filtering in, oyster-gray, through the long bay of leaded windows, falling sideways on the smiling faces, her beloved aunt and uncle, freckled May and long-chinned George, the sleek fair hair of Jeff's bowed head, her elated father and untroubled mother, Pamela in moss-green...

The room's Oriental effects had recently given way to English and French, not only as a result of passing fashion but of Jack's widening horizons, his trips abroad, his love affair with France. And Faith's eyes (or Tony Pemberton's), traveled across the expanse of rose-colored carpet to the dull rose-colored wallpaper, its gold tracery faintly shimmering, and the towering romantic painting, darkened by time, of a ruined English abbey, and the little seventeenth-century Dutch landscapes, glowing like jewels. In a lamplit corner there were chrysanthemums, also the color of ashes-of-roses.

She felt the sense of privilege one gets from looking into the interior of a van Eyck, rich with somber color and domestic detail. Her eyes, her imagination, widened suddenly into a vision of all living rooms on this Thanksgiving Day, the same pallid light illuminating them, and all Novembers, past and future, English and Dutch, and again she felt the welling up of incommunicable love, which at this moment included even herself, a loving clairvoyance, a wonder at her own genius, a tender omnipotence. Oh yes, Tony would admire, would love her, too!

Then Freda came to the door to announce dinner, and Faith discovered her goblet was empty, that she had sipped it away without minding its bitterness. She felt an odd regret, already a nostalgia, for her first drink, a milestone passed, for the glowing revelation of the familiar room, holding the people dearest to her, also fading from vision to memory, for a height from which she must descend.

Getting to her feet, she felt loose-jointed and graceful. The others, she realized, had been offered a second drink but she and Pamela had not. Perhaps that was part of her regret.

Aunt Grace and Uncle Severance were the first to leave at five o'clock. They never dallied, but quietly put on their coats and hats, said their goodbyes and were gone. The Morrisons lingered half an hour or so, but then they too rose to go. In a last aside, Faith whispered to Pamela, "Do you think Jeff would take us to the movies?" But Pamela made a comical face, rolling her eyes and hunching her shoulders, meaning, Who knows, with Jeff? She was obviously not concerned about a letdown; she would cross the street with her family to their cozy house and finish the evening sprawled across her mother's bed, where Faith had often found her—sharing confidences, foolishly laughing and eating peanut brittle.

The front door closed and Clara, exhaling a great sigh like an Amen, retired to her room and her crossword puzzle. Jack went up to his study to read—history, novels, textbooks, poetry: books were as necessary to him as food. A silence of great density settled on the house.

Faith sat perfectly still on one of the sofas by the grate fire. It was only a little past six and she put off going to her own room, where an inevitable despondency awaited her. Her ears rang. She rose and wandered about with her hands clasped behind her back. Stopping at the piano, she quietly played at random a page of Chopin (when she played Beethoven her father would shout, "For God's sake, less fortissimo!"), but she could never manage the airy elaborations and she gave up and went back to the sofa. She lit a cigarette, knowing perfectly well that *they* knew, upstairs, she was smoking.

Had Grace and Severance reached home by now? She pictured Severance removing his driving gloves, helping Grace off with her gray squirrel coat and hanging it for her, putting his overcoat away neatly, as he did everything, then going at once to the telephone to call the hospital . . . Faith had spent the night with them and knew how they lived, considerately, almost in silence, their needs known to each other, their lives closely bound, for they were childless . . .

The coals beside her burned watchfully. Her father had turned off most of the lamps and the room was darkened. The stillness overhead, too, was vigilant, the two figures like mythic gods in their separate chambers creating a heavy pervasion, all-knowing, inexorable.

When the telephone rang and Arthur Knox asked if she were doing anything, she almost cried out with relief. "Oh, Arthur, no, I'm not!" He was taken aback; she had so often refused him. He was an old Beechwood standby ("good old Arthur"), inclined to plumpness. Even in her wallflower days she had felt patronizing toward him. And although she knew he was close with money, she continued boldly, as Pamela might have done, "I was about to die of suffocation! What do you say we go to the movies?"

They sat in the loges of a vast gilded Loew's in a neighboring town and endured the stage show which always preceded the movies, a dismal succession of acrobats, tap-dancers, singers and time-worn comedians.

The movie, with Warner Baxter, was no less tedious. Arthur Knox held Faith's hand damply. The backs of his spongy fingers were pink with tiny pink pores. The Depression, which had hastened his father's death and forced him to leave college and take over his father's business, had all but made an old man of him. He supported his mother and sisters stoically, and seldom laughed. He wore his father's gold signet ring and drove his father's great Packard sedan.

Faith, still holding despair at bay, gazed upward at the cavernous gilded reaches of the theater, examined the minarets and tiny balconies, the wrought iron, the dim orange lights in lanterns, the stars glinting in the vaulted blue of the ceiling, and wished it were Tony Pemberton beside her.

Had anyone ever emerged from behind those dusty draperies onto those balconies, peeped out of those minarets? It was a theater she had been coming to since childhood and it had once seemed a fairyland, the Baghdad of Douglas Fairbanks, the palace of Maxfield Parrish paintings. Now she knew it was vulgar and fake and dirty.

Timidly Arthur put his arm around her and unthinkingly Faith leaned her head against his shoulder. At once she was aroused and comforted and, strangely, sadder than ever.

They headed homeward at last in Arthur's Packard, something of an antique ark even then. Everyone laughed at Arthur's car and his devoted care of it, although not unkindly, for they couldn't help admiring its majestic interior, its aristocratic odor, the soft synchronization of its motor and the way Arthur drove it, with the utmost caution, sometimes whispering to it.

There was no heater (one used rugs) and their breath steamed in the frosty night. Arthur said, "Sit closer," and Faith, exhausted, grateful for an old friend, slid closer.

The upstairs lights were out in the Farrell house. Arthur asked, "May I come in for a minute?"

Apprehensive now about his intentions, she fidgeted. "Well, just for a minute." It would be rude, after he had taken her to the movies, to refuse him. But in the downstairs hall, she whispered, "I'm starved, aren't you? It's been ages since we had dinner. Let's have a glass of milk." The kitchen, she thought, might be less conducive to amorous advances.

They stole quietly through the dining room and pantry, closing the doors behind them, smothering laughter. Faith went to the icebox. Behind the milk bottle was a Mason jar containing a small amount of orange liquid; she might have known—Freda never threw anything away, not even little dabs of oatmeal.

Faith seized the jar. "Look!" she whispered, whirling about, her face alight. "It's what's left of the cocktails we had today. Let's finish it."

There was an instant's silence. Arthur's plump face pouted. "Thanks, I'd rather have milk."

"Oh, Ar-thur! Come on, be a sport!"

He stared at her skeptically, a little embarrassed, as if she were playing a part. And she was! Myrna Loy, for instance, slim in black velvet, insouciant, brittle, invulnerable, or Joan Crawford, the madcap with the warm courageous heart, disappointed in love, defying gods.

She found the silver goblets in the pantry. "I don't know, maybe it's just orange juice. No, *phew*, it's got gin in it all right. Isn't this sinful? Come on, Arthur, you've *got* to have one." She divided the liquid, only half a glass apiece. "There. Now we have to make a toast. No, I tell you what, we'll make a wish. We'll each make a silent wish." She closed her eyes. *I wish that Tony*—No, something even more important than that. *I wish I may BE somebody. I wish I may get out of this house and BE somebody.*

She glanced at Arthur over the rim of the cup. He was still looking doubtful, disappointed, twirling his goblet in his fingers. She drank. It didn't taste bitter this time, it was familiar and welcoming, and perhaps it was this second drink she had been wanting all evening.

Her father stood in the kitchen doorway.

He was wearing his red silk robe, his left front eyetooth showing, which happened only with his greatest fury, his left shoulder lifted and twitching, his fingers twitching.

Without a word he stepped forward, snatched the gob-

28

let from Faith's hand, seized her wrist, dragged her to the sink. Arthur's stunned face bobbed like a balloon as her father whirled her around. And grasping the nape of her neck sharply in one hand, he thrust her head downward and washed out her mouth with soap.

She stumbled backward. Arthur had fled. She wiped her face with the back of her arm and hand. Soap and water ran down onto her velvet dress; it was ruined and it didn't matter. Her father had put his hands in the pockets of his robe. His face was crimson, he was furious and frightened. She must somehow vomit out the feeling of his fingers fumbling obscenely in her mouth. "I hate you, goddamn you. I hate you."

She had never said or even dared to think such a thing in her life. It was a blasphemy, god-shattering. He danced in her ragged vision as if he had cracked into fragments; his shoulders sloped, he was smaller.

It pleased him. She saw the tiny leap of delight in his eyes. The swinging door groaned and her mother burst into the kitchen wearing her old quilted maroon robe, her scalp showing through her unpinned hair.

"What is it, what, what—?"

He was delighted to tell her. "She was *drinking* with Arthur Knox." Her mother actually shrieked. "She has cursed me." His eyes never left Faith's face, he was feasting on her outrage.

"No. No. Faith. No. How dare you." Helplessly Clara stared at Faith, a childlike horror whitening her face.

"I don't care," Faith answered, her mouth soap-slimed. "I don't care!"

She didn't know what she might say because now she was free to say anything, and it was her body, obliterating her mind, that had revolted, that shook as if chilled, that struggled to uphold itself, that in some recess of itself insisted it was proud, delicate, feminine, graceful. The kitchen light was yellow, the cream-colored moldings around the cupboards reflected light, winking, and the two shrunken people before her were disgraced—her father and mother, disgraceful in their bathrobes, disheveled, loathsome, pathetic. "Go to hell, both of you, go to hell!"

Slam: the back of her mother's hand across her mouth, the wedding ring bruising her lips once more. "How. Dare. You. Don't. You. Ever."

"You go to your room." Her father's fingers bit into her shoulder. "You go to your room and stay there until we say you—"

She scrambled away from him. "I will not. I will not."

"As long as you live in our house you will obey us!"

"Then I'll leave, I won't *stay* here—!"

It was a dream. She was scrambling through the house, tipping up carpets; she had flung open the front door, she was out in the frosty night. "Faith, Faith," her mother was whimpering, panicky, pitiful, running after her down the sidewalk. "Come back, come back."

Where could she go, late at night, without a coat or hat—where could she go? Faith let her mother catch up, clutch her arm and draw her back to the house.

Jack Farrell waited nervously at the foot of the stairs. It had gone far enough. "Go to your room," he said mechanically, in a high voice.

"Now stop, Jack, stop it, I say. I won't have any more of this." He was relieved to give over to Clara. "Go to bed, Faith, we'll have no more of this. Go to bed and not another word from anyone."

Faith ran up the stairs and they stood watching her in silence.

She slammed the door and fell across the bed, her stomach hollowed, her brain heaving with blotted particles, pieces of herself, of her father and mother, of hatred. They were inseparable, interwoven, and she had done herself to death with them. She had wiped out her childhood. She longed to be a child again.

2

Faith married Tony Pemberton when she was twenty.

For years he had teasingly flirted with her; she had never outgrown the status of a friend of his younger sister. After graduating from St. Anne's and beginning to study seriously at the Arts Students' League, she saw less of him, for he was now a member of a downtown law firm and had his own apartment elsewhere in the city. She was thankful. Whenever she met him, his indulgent, impervious gallantry caused her a bout of misery.

Unwittingly she had become his sister's confidante. Mrs. Pemberton, a Peter Arno figure of a *grande dame*, kept Janice under her thumb in a far more Victorian regimen that Faith had even suffered. Janice was never allowed out of the house without a chaperone, had never taken a bus or a subway. Even when she was a senior at St. Anne's her mother's chauffeur waited for her every afternoon in the school's lobby, sometimes with a pair of rubbers in hand. She had few friends. But Mrs. Pemberton approved of Faith's exemplary manners, and Faith, who couldn't bear anyone's suffering loneliness, became a frequent visitor to their house. Despite her mother's tyranny, Janice had a genuine sweetness which made her all the more appealing. She was a doll-like girl, with small sloping shoulders, fluffy blond hair and china-blue eyes. She dimpled, showing her tiny teeth in a silent giggle, and was given to exploring occult religions. She was secretly corresponding with a dashing Englishman she had met on a Mediterranean cruise (properly chaperoned, of course, by an aunt), and she reported the romance, step by step, to Faith. It was a one-sided trust; Faith couldn't bring herself to confide her lonely passion for Tony.

When the Pembertons decided in their imperial way to give Janice a New Year's Eve Party, Faith accepted fatalistically, knowing Tony would be there, knowing how he would look in white tie and tails, sandy hair boyishly polished, blue eyes smiling, as he bent attentively over a lady, young or old, like a figure in a Regency drawing, how his foolish quips would fall, masking his intelligence and his sense of duty. She knew she would be at the mercy of her awareness of him every moment, his presence in a room or his absence distracting her, draining her, rendering her incapable of giving her full attention to anyone else. A terrible way to begin the new year!

The Pembertons' house on East 90th Street was filled with decorous young couples. One couldn't be anything else but decorous in this mahogany-paneled house, under Mrs. Pemberton's discriminating eye (although Mr. Pemberton was apt to get a little tight and squeeze the girls with more than fatherly affection). All of Faith's old St. Anne friends were there, and old beaus of friends, dancing in the drawing room, playing bridge in the library, nibbling sandwiches and sipping champagne in the dining room, frisking mildly on the stairs. And Tony moved among them as Faith had expected; he ranged from group to group, never giving anyone too much of himself and keeping an unobtrusive eye out for his mother's needs or a momentarily abandoned girl. A slight cowlick lifted his hair, but his boyishness was deceptive; no one so charming, so at ease, so detached, thought Faith with unaccountable logic, could fail to have a mistress tucked away somewhere. No wonder he had got out from under his mother's surveillance.

All at once Faith was weary of her attraction to him. It had gone on too long, she was sick of her own hopeless worship, and cynically she wearied of his elusive unyielding charm as well. She had an extra glass or two of champagne; she knew by now that alcohol had a fortuitous effect on her, that it cast out nervousness and released her from the blurred anxious person she thought herself to be and so distressingly often was.

Her sudden resignation gave her an uncommon splendor. She danced relaxedly, looking tall, lustrous, and regal in her bias-cut white satin gown, and faintly tragic, or devil-may-care. She wore a circlet of brilliants over her russet hair, and her face, turned away from Tony, the lines of cheekbones and jaw, were cool and lovely. She had no more need to laugh superfluously as some of the other girls did, but she could smile a dazzling smile.

The young men were impressed (and how young they suddenly seemed!), and Tony, too, cut in often. Strangely, he dropped his frivolous talk, and holding her firmly, danced with her in silence.

At midnight he worked his way to her, took her by the elbows and kissed her lightly but unhurriedly on the lips. Under the festive clamor around them he said, "Faith, I've fallen in love with you," and although the deep healthy blue of his eyes danced with smiling lights, he looked grief-stricken.

They swayed slightly to the impromptu singing of "Auld Lang Syne," touching each other's elbows, and she answered with an unflustered smile, "Well, at last. I thought you'd never get around to it." They stood swaying, staring, laughing at each other.

It was several days before he telephoned her. And again his delay seemed to her elusive, tantalizing; or perhaps he had had second thoughts. And sure enough, when he did call he sounded as mock-foolish as ever, light and liberal of tongue, an astute and up-and-coming attorney disguised as a perennial Princetonian, and she thought: O God, he's telling me he wasn't serious!

But in the ruby dimness of the Pembertons' box at the Metropolitan, while Kirsten Flagstad poured clarion song over the prostrate form of Lauritz Melchior, Tony took her hand and pressed it to his lips. Then, holding it down between them, he crushed it, shaking it protestingly, or impatiently, and wouldn't let go.

"Yes, but they shouldn't *lunge*," she said languidly as they drove uptown to supper at the Plaza. "When they lunge across the stage at each other you have to make yourself believe in *corpulent* gods."

And this unlikely statement seemed to confirm something for him. Instead of turning right on Central Park South he headed without explanation straight into the cold and dark-branched park (he was driving his own small coupe), pulled up to the curb on a remote rise, and with both hands drew her face to him. "Faith, will you marry me?"

She never questioned his suddenness, or asked herself who, exactly, she was marrying.

He was simply the ideal, the unattainable prince, the fair-haired boy. Even her parents admired him. He was proof of herself. He was the answer. He was escape from the suffocation of the Beechwood house, from despair, from the unlovely child—another escape that sealed its own door behind her.

"But even if I had known," she told Dr. Pomeroy, "what it was going to be like, being married to Tony, how I had romanticized him, and what *I* was going to be like, being married to him—I still would have had to do it."

But why Tony had chosen her, among all the well-born, becomingly wayward girls he knew—the dashing Vassar graduates, the brainy career girls (one even a lawyer), the sexually proficient "older women"—was a mystery to Faith. His handsomeness, his intellect, his upbringing, so much more patrician, she believed, than her own, were more than she deserved, she of the lifelong brown shadow. He loved her, he told her so, he still told her so after their marriage, sometimes with tears in his eyes, exposing a need in himself that disconcerted her. They frolicked joyously in and on their double bed; often he came home somewhat sheepishly at noon to be with her for half an hour, to make love. They loved each other, there was no doubt of that in her mind; they loved each other more as time passed than in the beginning.

But who, she marveled, *who* was he in love with? She begged him to tell her.

He said, "I always liked you enormously. In fact, you rather fascinated me. But, well, it just never occurred to me that— this—was possible. And when it did, New Year's Eve, there was simply no question about it. There couldn't be anyone else."

36

Still that didn't tell her what she wanted to know, and she recognized in him an obscure reluctance to discuss his feelings for her. She ceased to press him. He could talk less freely about his feelings for her than he could of his last mistress, of whom she was wildly jealous; and his reticence about his attraction to Faith made her jealous in almost the same way, as if it implied she was prying, forcing him to discuss a woman whom, since she didn't know her, she had no right to know.

"You needed to feel you were worthwhile," Dr. Pomeroy told her. "You needed him to tell you so."

"And that would make anybody uncomfortable, wouldn't it?" she agreed. "It would make anyone resist. If I hadn't needed to know it so desperately, he might have told me." She frowned. "But it was more than that. He would put on such a mystifying smile. Maybe he felt that telling me would give me an unfair advantage over him."

For as time passed she began to sense a schism between what was evident—their avowed and demonstrated love for each other—and what was concealed: a confused background of unmentioned superiorities and tolerated inadequacies, an obscure contest in which gratuitous points were justly withheld and failures scored, an uneasy balance in which she was constantly outweighed.

She felt her own good looks evaporating, eclipsed by Tony's. Even while his private love for her deepened, he became outwardly oblivious of her, as if this too were a balance. They were invited to a good many parties by his old friends, and she was well aware (just possibly encouraged by Tony to be aware) that he, their erstwhile favorite bachelor, was the one they really wanted. In an anxious attempt to be "pretty" she dressed in the then-fashionable tailored suit and blouse with ruffled jabot; he made no comment, and she wondered if the costume was becoming to her. She felt lost in the cocktail party uproar. Tony, who was usually on the far side of the room from her, seemed once again unattainable, almost a stranger. She smiled and smiled, she strained to keep her attention on the company near her, she tried to be amusing. And when they left, Tony was gratified and chatty, while she was gray, dull, faceless and nameless.

"When you feel unattractive," said Dr. Pomeroy, uttering one of his unpalatable truths, which had the effect of settling in some way the responsibility upon herself, "you *are* unattractive."

Of her own friends, Tony liked only two: the subtle, waspish Mrs. Bent-Ufford from St. Anne's, whom Faith had never stopped seeing, and gay May Morrison. The rest he suggested she entertain when he was at work. She realized then that she had a number of very close cronies, haphazardly acquired over the years, while Tony had no one as close and wanted none. He kept his friends at arm's length, where he felt in his meticulous way they properly belonged.

As for Faith's painting, he encouraged it and expressed admiration for certain canvases, but he apparently did not take pride in it. He never mentioned it to his friends and never suggested she hang a painting in their apartment. She realized that painting, even painting well, was in his circle not an especially commendable accomplishment, and that he would have been prouder of her if she had been able to play tennis well or ski.

Intuition told her it was in part her very creativity which had captivated him, and she could still make him burst into laughter at her fanciful slant on things, but his lawyer's mind put to shame the cloudy place that functioned as a mind for her. She had never had an aptitude for facts and figures, and she was dismayingly inefficient as a household manager, forgetful, timid with tradespeople. She tried to make a joke of it, quoting Milne: "I am a Bear of Very Small Brain." He smiled and did not contradict her.

He tried reeducating her. He weaned her away from the *Herald-Tribune* and set her to work reading the editorials and speeches-in-full in the *Times*, just as he persuaded her to drink Scotch and soda rather than rye and ginger ale. He made her keep a budget and went over it every Sunday. He tried teaching her tennis and skiing, but her coordination, he told her, smiling and shaking his head, was hopeless. In time he gave up his efforts; it was a lost cause.

But it was Tony's unconscious snobbery that most clearly came to light and which most diminished her. His parents were true upper-middle-class *bourgeoisie* (a word they themselves thought was used only by Bolsheviks). They were militantly Republican; they kept old-fashioned maids who gave impeccable service; they disapproved of Tony's sometimes casual dress or careless use of the English language; they never had to think twice about right and wrong and could tell at a glance who were "nice" people.

Tony, perhaps by dint of the advantages they had provided, or perhaps simply by right of his many attributes, was more purely aristocratic. He was unfailingly courteous to Faith's family and friends, impenetrably charming, but she knew they all, all, belonged to a category of slightly rumpled, wholesome, gifted or conscientious people who were meaningless to him. Her father's fame, her Uncle Severance, failed to impress him. Even though they were both now in *Who's Who*, as his own father was not, they lacked a certain ingredient, a quality which, if one possessed it, made all the difference, molded one's life—one's schooling, one's speech, one's clubs, one's sports, one's haircut, even the shape of one's skull.

Once, during their engagement, Tony had asked Faith, embarrassed at himself, embarrassed for her, or because of her, "Will you mind being in the Social Register?"

Mrs. Pemberton bestirred herself to get Faith into the Junior League and the Cosmopolitan Club, but after the first introductory tea—which Faith endured with the ingratiating smile stiffening her face and her ordinary no-class accent changing to match the slurred drawls around her—a terrible shamed panic mounted in her, and she wailed, "Tony, I can't! I hate clubs! Women's clubs! I just *can't!*"

"But, darling, they're very *nice* women, and you should have a club—"

"*Why?* I'd never set foot in the place!" Distress filled her voice, and she saw the disappointment, the dawning acceptance in Tony's face. "Oh, Tony, I'm sorry, but I'm just not *like* that!"

She looked up from her book one Sunday evening, with the autumn rain pattering on the flagstones of their little Sutton Place garden and the lights of the Queensboro Bridge shining out of the gathering dusk, and felt, once more, despair.

The world's wet Sunday-grief swept up from the past to surround her, engulf her, and the old yearning pulled her down.

"Tony!" she called.

"Yes, dear?"

"Come in here and sit with me!"

"I can't, dear. I'm working on my accounts. It's my only chance, on Sunday."

What did she want? She was married to Tony Pemberton, she had escaped Beechwood; she had everything she had ever dreamed of. Then what was it she lacked?

She got up quietly and went down the hall to the little extra bedroom Tony used as den, library and dressing room. He was in his shirt sleeves, leaning forward over his desk, the green lamplight silhouetting his neat head and suave nape. She went up behind him and enfolded his chest in her arms, softly pressing her breast against the back of his head. "Tony?"

"Yes, dear?" He called her *dear* when she interrupted him.

"Tony . . ." She rested her cheek against his smooth light-brown hair without rumpling it. His fragrance—hair, skin, broadcloth—intoxicated and terrified her, so winning, so unpossessable. "Oh, I love you, Tony."

"I love you too, dear." He turned to her, not smiling, his fine features sleepy-looking with annoyance, his blue eyes still in their account-book focus. "But I'm trying to work." He took her hands, disengaging her arms. "*Please* let me finish. I'll only be a little while."

"I'm sorry, darling." She retreated. Something snarled and knotted in her. In a mood like this she wanted to read his old love letters, look at snapshots of his old girls, tear up her own drawings. She moved to his dresser. "Why do you have to have Kent brushes?" she demanded, abrading his snob-faith, his unquestioning devotion to labels: Kent, Peel, Upmann, Brooks Brothers, Abercrombie

& Fitch, S.S. Pierce, Steuben, Cartier; Tuxedo Park, Bar Harbor, Westbury—on and on, endless codifications looming like totem poles over his conduct. "Where do they get their bristles from anyway—White Russian pigs?"

"Of course not," he answered mildly. "They grow them, didn't you know that?" He was leaning over his work again. "Acres and acres of them. Haven't you heard the old song, 'When It's Bristletime in Kent?' "

She turned, breaking into laughter. Just when, caught in her own iron vise, she considered him impossible, irredeemable, he disarmed her, disarming himself. This, she believed, was the real Tony, however transitory, the original child whom no one had totemized, darting among the pillars of his upbringing and showing his face just long enough for her to believe in him.

"Oh, Tony, you're adorable sometimes!" He smiled, too, absently, appreciating her laughter. She said, "I guess I'll make myself a cup of tea. Would you like a cup of tea?"

"No, thank you."

"Shall we have cocktails? Would you like to have cocktails tonight?" They rarely drank together except when they were entertaining or being entertained. They had tried it and it hadn't worked out very well. Faith's anticipation of a glowing hour, an hour of enclosing themselves in delving into their own delightful wellsprings as the one or two martinis pacified and liberated them (she actually had a happy foreglimpse of herself and Tony seated in the lamplight of their living room), never materialized. The drinks seemed to distill the limbo between them, and the unreal obscurities of their lives became real. Tony was apt to say things he later regretted. ("No, we will *not* have children." The little smile. "Not until

I say so. Maybe never.") It was as if Faith, by anticipating closeness, automatically prohibited it.

"No," he told her now curtly. "No cocktails."

"Oh." Her finger trailed over the edge of his dresser, left it, fell. It was unfair, she felt, that cocktails changed him from pleasant to unpleasant, and herself from unpleasant to pleasant. He made her suggestion—without meaning to, of course—appear dishonorable. "All right then. I'll make myself a cup of tea."

"*Do*," he said, his patience almost exhausted.

She left him at last, went down the hall to the little kitchen. She felt gray again, and nameless. Their one bottle of Scotch faced her when she opened a cabinet for the teabags. She took it down without thinking, reached for a glass from the drainboard and poured herself a strong drink, which she diluted with water. *The hell with you*, she said in silence, without meaning anyone in particular. And while the teakettle came to a boil she gulped down the drink. Then, a little dazed, her eyes watering, she carried her teacup to the living room, a secret smile spreading her lips.

The day changed, of course, the world changed. Herself, who had been lost (abandoned, rejected—Sundayed), awoke, reinhabited her veins. How nice, how snug, to be sipping hot sugary tea on a Sunday evening in her own little house (*their* little house!) while the rain pattered outside. How beautiful the bridge was, its lights soaring! Could she paint it? A dark undercoat (marine-blue? violet-blue?) and an overcoating of burnt umber, thinly spread with a knife and streaked with blue, red, to give the breathing vitality of wetness, and then the fogged lights, lemon, magenta . . . Of course she could paint it, it would simply pour out of her fingers—magnificently!

I don't *care*, she told herself; I'll do it again sometime, when I'm feeling low. Just one drink, and no harm done! But she wished she dared have another. Inevitably she wished it.

"Oh God, what a bore I was," she moaned to Dr. Pomeroy, for by the time she got to him the self-pity was at its worst. "What a trial. What a drag on Tony. What a dead weight. Given the same conditions I might have done better, if only I had had the least ounce of self-respect!"

"You know, Faith," said Tony's mother, looking sad and top-heavy, as she did when dispensing advice, "there is a tremendous adjustment for newly married couples to make." She had chalk-white skin and a long sloping white nose paralleling her long pear-shaped bosom. "The first two years are the hardest."

Faith dropped her eyes, studying her hands. What had Mrs. Pemberton read in her face? Clichés uttered by Mrs. Pemberton had a comforting and strangely foreign quality, like some universal truth translated from the Chinese. The hushed paneled library in which they sat, with its conventional appointments—bound volumes, jade ashtrays, bronze statuettes, Mr. Pemberton's green leather wing chair, all in such good bad-taste, or such bad good-taste—had the same quality. In the Pemberton house Faith felt safe, buttressed, yet alien.

Janice was in London, visiting her aunt and no doubt carrying on her illicit romance.

"Men are apt to be selfish creatures," continued Mrs. Pemberton omnisciently—she who had properly cowed

Mr. Pemberton, "and one must learn a great deal of patience in dealing with them."

Faith's conversations with Mr. Pemberton usually took place hurriedly in corners of a room, or on the stairs, as if their affection for each other was a conspiracy. He had a swarthy, heavily lined face and wore old-fashioned suits tightly buttoned over a little paunch. "Is there anything you need?" he would whisper. "Anything I can do? Please don't hesitate to ask."

They were gathered in Shem Faber's studio—Faith, some painters, Shem's girl friend, who was a writer of children's books, and one anonymous musician. Tony was tied up all evening on a legal matter and Faith had taken the opportunity to come downtown alone. The studio was an immense, lofty room, nearly forty feet long, chalk-colored, stark and serene, with a gray paint-spattered floor —so spacious that it made even a dozen people seem a a small group. They sat in a circle around a daybed covered with yellow canvas, a woolly Greek rug under their feet and a white pitcher of jonquils on the model's platform that served as a coffee table. There were no paintings or posters on the bleached walls. Shem's tall canvases leaned there, back-to, neatly stacked. At the end opposite the door he kept his equipment—the towering easel and the worktables and a spattered screen around a sink.

Shem was a chubby, gentle young man, generous, hard-working; he had little to say to anyone but he was always smiling. It was Shem, one night when they were playing a game of acting-out painters, who had darted up a stepladder, turned his back and let down his trousers, baring his round bottom, and said softly, "Rubens!" It was

45

understood that one could drop in on him any evening, or rather, drop in on his studio, for Shem usually continued about his business in the background.

In the circle they were chatting and smoking, drinking tea and beer, the three or four painter friends stretched out in folding canvas chairs and the girls seated on the daybed. Mona, Shem's girl, was telling them about the nice policeman who had stopped at her basement apartment to scold her for not covering her window and stayed to fix the Venetian blind. Her fine blond hair fell about her face in untidy whisps, and her mind was like her hair: fine, highlighted, draped with trust and quaint ideas, which she voiced like blank verse in hesitant, oddly chosen words, interspersed with laughter. Everyone thought she was too gifted to confine her writing to children's books, but she laughed and kept on turning them out, dozens of them, publishing under several pen names.

The half-reclining painters, who couldn't be still for long, took over the talk, waving their arms, but the dark-clothed musician remained silent, his black violin case hugged close to his feet like a valise, as if he had just got off the boat from Estonia or Portugal and didn't speak English. And all the while Shem smiled and puttered in the background, scrubbing things at his sink, arranging them on his worktable, moving about lightly on sneakered feet.

He and his friends always welcomed Faith. Shem showed her a special courtesy, sometimes bowing gravely over her hand like a boy at dancing school, and Mona cried, "Oh, here's our dream girl!" meaning someone not of their dreams but with mysterious dreams of her own. Since Mona assigned her this romantic role, Faith felt herself filling it, wafting in on them from her circumspect world.

Perhaps she did after all give something, however unwittingly, for she was in love with Shem's studio and his circle of friends, and she reflected back to them something of themselves. She spoke little, preferring to listen, absorbing every offhand word and gesture, every detail of the wonderful great room, its workmanlike grace, its cool changing light and its radiants of lemon-yellow. It was this charmed admiration that overcame their initial doubts of her, her refined dress and orthodox diamond ring, and touched the pulse of their own self-belief, quickening their aspirations. They had seen nothing of her work and didn't want to. The fact that she painted at all, badly or well, seemed part of her myth—their ladylike, amorphous dream girl.

Someone asked the musician to play. Without a word, as impersonal as a plumber, he took up his case, carefully opened it, extracted his violin and briefly tested it—a few hoarse, inquiring notes, a twist or two of a knob. Tenderly he settled the instrument under his chin, held his breath for an instant, during which his heavy eyes seemed to recede, and then he commenced to play.

The fluid, ink-dark voice leaped vividly into the air, leaving a trail of Bach's parallels, spirals and interlacery, like a diagram of energy itself, exuberant yet perfectly ordered, astonishing the vacant reaches of the studio, crowding it with evanescent calligraphy.

Shem stood transfixed at his worktable. Mona, her arms folded on her knees, studied her feet. The others, quelled, lay motionless. The player himself, pale, rapt, remote, watched like a conjuror as his fluctuating arm and dancing fingers propelled the invisible inventions into being.

And Faith thought: How lowly, the indomitable skiers, the proficient tennis players! How drab and empty the well-shaped skulls, how pompous the long noses, the whole company of "nice" people, dumb and subservient, like well-bred horses. How essentially vulgar. How boring!

These were the true aristocrats: the artists, the pioneers, the unfettered!

Perhaps that was her difficulty. She was an anomaly, neither fish nor fowl. There had been contradictions all along the way, beginning with her upbringing by the last of the Victorians—prudish mother, tyrannical father—in an increasingly Freud-enlightened world. Now she found herself yet again with her feet in two camps, Shem's and the Pembertons', almost as opposite as true and false. She belonged totally in neither one of them. In both of them she betrayed something of herself. No wonder, she told Dr. Pomeroy later on, she had such confused standards, such delusions of grandeur, such setbacks and reversals, such despair!

"Maybe my whole life," she brooded aloud to him, "has been a search for reconciliation."

She had been married two years when her mother and father were divorced and he married Violet Hovis, his secretary and long-time mistress, and the Beechwood house was sold.

Faith believed thankfully when she married Tony that she was leaving the Beechwood house behind her forever, but in fact she was forever haunted by it, and after it was sold, when she knew she would never set foot in it again, it began to present itself in her dreams, exact in every detail and color, the setting for endless parables, for moods and actions which had no apparent connection with the house at all. Sometimes it became the background for violence:

once in a nightmare she stabbed her father there.

Just before the house was to be occupied by the new tenants, after her mother had left it, Faith awakened in the middle of the night and knew with horror how it was at that very moment: walked in her imagination through its empty rooms and on up into the empty upstairs hall, the light from the streetlamp glimmering through the vacant windows. She knew at that moment the deserted house was filled with a listening stillness, with the absence of its familiar sounds, chronic creaks of certain stair treads, faucets running, the groan of the pantry door, voices . . . listening, listening . . .

Her mother rented an apartment in the city near Faith, where, crushed by the divorce, the rejection, she sank into a paralysis of sorrow. In vain Faith tried to console, to reassure, to divert her, telephoning her every morning, seeing her every day, persuading Tony to take them to dinner and the movies on weekends. The loneliness of anyone, friend or stranger, caused in Faith a surge of outrage, an intolerable compassion, like that of seeing an animal mistreated. Alone, she gave way to gusts of weeping for her mother. She couldn't enjoy an evening without her for thinking of her solitary misery. She kept a kind of emotional watch over her, day and night.

Her mother could not or would not be consoled. She sat unbudgingly downcast while Tony, at dinner, bravely tried to lure her into small talk. Her shoulders remained abject, her mouth drawn downward between two deep lines, her voice, when she was forced to speak, a murmur squeezed from the stomach of her despondency. Indeed, Faith was aware of her mother's irritation at their attempts to cheer her, and although Tony maintained an inscrutable patience, Faith sometimes lost her own.

She couldn't help recognizing an awful justice in the

divorce. The picture of her mother playing solitaire day after day in her bedroom at the Beechwood house had always troubled her, and its morose complacency, the self-sufficiency of her mother's plainness, as if she claimed un-adornment as a virtue, the implicit resentment of her great slump, enraged Faith, and now she wanted to shake her, shout at her: What did you expect? You *couldn't* have loved him, wearing those untidy brown sweaters and skirts, those clodhoppers and polo coats. You don't love him even now, refusing to speak to him or see him ever again, referring to him as *"your* father." It's only your pride that's been hurt! You are not alone, you have a sister, relatives and loyal friends, and me just down the street—yes, even me! Are you punishing us?

Then her mother asked her point-blank, in tears, "Do you think it was my fault? I couldn't bear to think it was my fault!" And Faith, realizing her mother's agony was real, whatever the cause, her life shattered when it was too late to start afresh, hastened to reply, Of course it wasn't!

It was at the end of this conversation that her mother added, as an afterthought, as if she were talking about bagpipe music or mushrooms, "I never cared for sex," and Faith was appalled at such dense self-righteousness. And it wasn't until after her own cataclysm and her delivery that she belatedly let herself hear the tremble of self-doubt in her mother's voice and the tiny note of mystification. Then she remembered the stories of little Grace's beautiful chestnut curls, and how on Sunday the sisters were forbidden to read fairy tales, and with these small clues, filled in the mute omissions of her mother's life.

There were times after her mother's divorce when Faith wondered what labyrinths—passages, turnings, mirrors—lay behind her own anguished solicitude. How could she yearn so over this lonely woman who, she believed, had never yearned over her, from whom, in fact, she herself had learned loneliness? She might have been a little girl still, trying to make up for her mother's scant love with obsessive offerings of love. She asked herself, too, why her mother had turned at once for comfort not to Grace or May Morrison but to Faith. Was it no more than the quality in Faith that made people trust her, or did Clara knowingly sense she had trained her daughter all her life to be her alter ego?

In her mother's tradition Faith refused to see her new stepmother. Tony, more objective, said, "Faith, this is silly. You'll have to see her. After all, she's your father's wife."

"I can't! All those years, carrying on with him!"

"Oh, Faith, really. 'Carrying on.' You told me yourself it wasn't a real marriage, hadn't been for years."

"She's broken my mother's heart!"

Tony sighed, opened his mouth to speak, thought better of it. He said in his level lawyer's tone, "Faith, try to look at the facts without emotion. Given a choice, would you deny your father's right to happiness and insist he continue living with your mother under the circumstances of their marriage?"

But she didn't dare let him reason with her. "Tony, she's devastated!"

"She'll get over it, darling. She *will* get over it."

"She'll never get over it!"

"She'll have to. She can't keep this up."

"Keep *what* up?" Faith cried warningly.

"You know what. It's six months since the divorce and she's still playing the wronged woman to the hilt."

"She's not playing!" Tears were running down Faith's

cheeks. "She's broken-hearted!" Were they having it out? Had Tony at last lost patience? And in spite of her tears and a furious feeling that he was stripping her of something, something that perhaps she, too, clung to, she felt a relief and a grateful closeness to him, the first in a long time. She gave way suddenly, piteously. "Oh, Tony, if only she *would* get over it!"

He smiled and put his arms around her and they clung to each other. "Dear girl, I know it's been hard on you—"

"It's been hard on you, too," she sobbed, "and you've been *so* good about it—"

"Nonsense." This was part of his dearness to her, his responsibility to others, his selflessness in time of stress, which made her conversely wish to comfort him. "Look." He took her hands, palms up, and frowned into her eyes. "I tell you what we're going to do. I have some business in Charleston, and we're going down there and see a little of the South, maybe as far as New Orleans—"

"Oh, but Tony, I can't leave M—"

"Oh yes you can. That's the whole point. You're going to get away. Make a break. And when we come back we're going to meet your father and Violet and you're going to stop mothering your mother—"

"Tony!" she exploded, beginning to laugh. "You're brilliant! Mothering my mother!"

"So you get some summer things out and I'll make the arrangements..."

But it was May Morrison who uttered the words that forced Clara out of her cave of despondency.

Very soon after her return from the South, before the meeting with her father and Violet, Faith insisted on entertaining her Uncle Severance and Aunt Grace, the Morrisons and, of course, Clara. Tony was not enthusiastic; perhaps he suspected this dinner was to be a tacit pledge to these favorite elders that they would always come first. Faith's disproportionate sentiments, so deeply rooted in the past, her ardent gestures, which she herself could not, or would not, understand, made him uncomfortable; anything he considered inordinate he also considered unseemly.

And the evening got off to an unpromising start. Severance roared too loudly and made his abominable puns; Grace shushed him; and May, trying to smooth things, crooned meaninglessly. They tried too hard to revive the spirit of the old Beechwood gatherings for the very reason that they were aware so much had changed. Jack, the touchstone, was missing; Pamela was away at college; Jeff was married and working for an insurance company in San Francisco. As cocktails progressed into dinner, Tony grew more and more inscrutably courteous and Clara more taciturn.

But after dinner it was Tony who saw to it that Severance was allowed for once to discourse in his serious, imaginative way, and on this new track everyone relaxed, giving up the frantic effort to steer the evening into something it could not be, and voices blended more harmoniously.

They were discussing unselfishness, and Severance argued that all unselfish acts had a selfish basis. Clara scornfully *hmphed*, as she often did at Severance. "That's not true," she declared flatly. And Faith, who had been punished time and again for her selfishness as a child, stirred uneasily, knowing her uncle's argument was a threat to her mother's reason for being. Clara had lived a lifetime of unselfishness.

And then May Morrison, hesitantly lilting, said, "Well, but there are different kinds of selfishness, don't you think? I had a school friend once who died, and her mother mourned her terribly, mourned her and mourned her and mourned her, never stopped mourning her, wore everyone out with her mourning, bored everyone to death. She became a trial to everyone. Now don't you think that was selfish?"

There was a tiny, quick silence, and Severance went on with his discourse, but Faith studied her hands, not daring to look up at her mother. Was there an ulterior motive in May's story?

The next day Clara was different. She looked as if she had put down a burden and felt refreshed in spite of herself. Her face was rested, surprised and vulnerable, like the face of someone who has survived a grave illness.

For all her hurt pride, she had swallowed the lesson of May's story. Perhaps the possibility of becoming a trial to everyone hurt her pride more than her abandonment by Jack; it didn't matter. Alone, through her own resolution, she had turned over a new leaf.

People changed, Faith realized, although the realization carried little weight at the time. They were not like Dickens *personnae*, always dependably in character, immutable to the last. The most stubborn, the most arrogant, the most helpless, the most unexpected of people could, and did, in midstream, if they were willing, change.

And she recognized a heroic quality in her mother, the quality of courage without insight. Faith shed tears for her again; her mother was more tragic in her self-restitution than in her misery.

Tony and Faith went at last to dinner with Violet and Jack in their new house in the city.

Faith was polite, pleasant and cool. Her father was so anxious to please her, to win her liking for his new wife, that some outer or inner layer of her stony heart quickened with pity. She wished she could forgive him, not only for her mother's anguish but for all the bygone humiliations to herself. But her mother's suffering was still too much a part of her, and she refused to be promoted to the position of someone who could no longer be humiliated, and thus must forgive. To embrace Violet and Jack in one fell swoop was simply asking too much of her. She had no idea how potent, how punishing, her coldness could be.

Violet, lovely in a brocaded gown, her golden hair arranged in braids around her head, her eyes appealing, despairing, bravely supported Jack, tirelessly sustaining the fragmented conversation. And again it was Tony who rose to the occasion and made the evening bearable, paying the proper compliments, making them laugh.

They were so proud of their house, and Faith resented it with an angry jealousy. It was one of the first brownstones to be remodeled in the modern style; pictures of it had already appeared in the *Times* and *House & Garden*. Enviously Faith took note of its elegant appointments, the vermeilled silver and heavy crystal and exquisitely embroidered linen, the magnificence of lighting, the rugs and furniture designed by Jack himself.

Faith and Tony had aimed high with their Steuben glass and Jensen silver, but this elegance was the fruit of her father's more immediate world of design and craftsmanship; these appointments had come from distant French and Italian ateliers where price was immaterial. Like Shem's studio, the house was filled with quiet beatitude, a kind of stern rapture. Her father's intelligent hands, tinted with red down, caressed the object, a plate or a bit of sculpture, as he described to Faith the artist, and tears mounted to his eyes, and wretchedly Faith longed to be as consistent, to live in such purity of purpose.

How happy it was, how splendid! How it outshone her mother's new apartment, which even with its fine southern view of the East River always managed to look dark. Certainly the Pembertons' platitudinous house couldn't hold a candle to it. Sick at heart, Faith observed how the white walls set off the English landscape and the little Dutch paintings. Jack and Violet were not name-droppers, but it was evident that they had, too, a glamorous social life, filled with dynamic people involved in creative enterprises, not only architectural but theatrical, literary and even political. With irrepressible enthusiasm, Jack recounted the commissions he was engaged in, the trips abroad to consult with foreign heads of state . . . How unfair!

Faith would come to look back on this evening with chagrin. It demanded some maturity of her, and she was brattish. It demanded some suavity, if not magnanimity, and she drank too much wine and vulgarly helped herself to Tony's after-dinner highball when she was not offered a refill. With patience, with special consideration, all her mentors, even including her mother, seemed to be asking her to capitulate, to take the giant step of adult forbearance, and she could not. She alone hung back churlishly, clinging to some childish indemnity of her own, some extreme ideal, savage and self-tormenting, as if in her life with them she had backed into a corner from which she could not safely move.

3

They had been married five years and the war had begun in Europe, when Faith decided to become pregnant without Tony's permission. To her surprise, he was delighted. Was it because she had taken the decision, the responsibility, out of his hands? She was healthier pregnant than at any time of her life, her hair and skin glowing, but it was her dependency that aroused his tenderness. ("Here is your early bird," he said, coming in with her breakfast tray, "bringing you worms.") They expected a boy, but they were overjoyed with a girl. Tony claimed he wouldn't take an interest in her until she was three, but as it turned out, he cherished the smiling infant almost as unconditionally as Faith did, and tears spilled down his cheeks when he held her for the last time.

. . .

Immediately after Pearl Harbor, Tony applied for a commission in the Navy, and eventually was sent to Hawaii. The following autumn Faith and the baby, Anne, moved into a larger apartment with her mother and Mona O'Neill, Shem's girl, for Shem had been drafted.

This wartime ménage did not begin, however, as a dreary household of forsaken women; on the contrary, it was enlivened by the pooling of their lives, and full of laughter, discussion, funny domestic crises. All kinds of friends dropped in, and there were pleasant evenings after the baby's bedtime when they settled down around the red velvet couch for sherry.

To begin with, everyone was intrigued by the apartment itself, in a house in the Seventies. The owners lived in the three top floors, and the women occupied the remodeled ground floor and basement. From the communal foyer one entered a spacious hall off the bedrooms, which had once been drawing rooms—high-ceilinged, with fireplaces and inside shutters; and then one went down into the basement to the living room, where French doors opened onto a garden, and the kitchen quarters. Together the three women could afford it, although individually their funds were limited. Faith and Mona labored to make it attractive out of combined resources—Shem's and Faith's paintings, a few good antiques from the Beechwood house, Mona's red velvet couch, Empire draperies fashioned out of black and white ticking bought at a sale at Bloomingdale's.

Clara looked on with amusement, half scornful and half mystified, as the younger women sewed yards and yards of ball fringe on the ticking. She had long ago lost interest in decoration and no longer bothered with curtains at her windows or rugs on her floor. When the girls gave a party Faith would steal into Clara's room at the last minute to pick up stockings draped over chairs, shoes or an old corset. "How you two do slave!"

"Some people *must* have pleasant surroundings!" Mona answered. She looked up, brushing aside her pale hair. She had the most reasonable and unobjectionable and fearless way of stating things. "I suppose it's a need to reflect yourself, like smiling at people to make them smile back."

And Clara gave a short laugh, as if to say *Touché!*

The things Mona uttered out of her honest ingenuousness were like benefactions to Clara, as if they came from an older blood-relative she respected, or a blameless child, and she enjoyed allowing herself to profit by them. All that Faith could not say bluntly and defiantly, Mona could say delightfully.

Their friendship surprised Faith. Not only were they far apart in age but, for one thing, Clara had to accept Mona's relationship with Shem, whatever it was, for Mona serenely felt no need to explain it. With anyone else, Clara's mere suspicion of an affair would have ended the friendship. And for another, Mona's relationship with humanity itself was the antithesis of Clara's. Mona doted on people with something of her Irishness, welcoming their quirks and perversities, never making antagonists of them with preconditioned judgments but relishing them for their very incorrigibility, as some wry-minded aunts have a charm over mischievous nephews. She was deaf to the bitter little digs at life Clara still couldn't resist voicing now and then, bringing all conversation to an awkward halt, which Faith found so punishing. When Clara frowned, Mona laughed. Mona even dared to laugh at Clara! It may have been that Mona unconsciously demonstrated how much kinder she was than the self-righteous, the "good" people of Clara's rigid upbringing. For gradually Mona brought out in the older woman a humor and temperateness, even a worldliness that astonished Faith.

The two of them, Mona and Clara, attended lectures at the Metropolitan Museum, and concerts, went water-coloring on the East River or in the park, and came home buoyant and wind-flushed. Clara's water colors showed a release of vitality they had never shown in her youth, when she dropped painting to take up the cares of wifehood.

If only she had been like this with Jack! Faith thought, marveling. But Clara seemed to have given up a contest, as if her morose passivity in Beechwood had actually been active, an embattlement in reverse, and now, relenting, having surrendered herself with a final sigh, a graciousness emerged. She watched and followed the talk and activities of the two younger women with amusement, she enjoyed the baby, she often sat smiling, half participant and half observer, like a pleased newcomer, her hands in repose.

They were all three united in polite and diverting warfare against the Mountforts, who owned the house and lived in the upper floors. The Mountforts had the thermostat, and the women below had the temperamental, antiquated furnace, an arrangement destined to generate conflict. Mr. Mountfort, pink and polished of face, a tall sly gentlemanly bird wearing a Racquet Club tie, made promises of repair he did not keep, excused all his derelictions on the premise of wartime conditions, and turned the thermostat down to sixty degrees in the winter when he and his family went away for the weekend. (They never bothered to lock inside doors in those days, and Faith simply went upstairs, located the thermostat in the Mountforts' darkened, many-mirrored living room and turned it up again.)

Mrs. Mountfort, tall also but more careworn, Bostonian of mien and accent, was seen only as a refined wraith, wringing her hands like Lady Macbeth at the top of her stairs and murmuring last-minute admonitions to her departing kin. Faith and Mona, who occupied the front bedroom adjoining the common foyer and could plainly hear through an unused door all the comings and goings of the upstairs family, were in awe of Mrs. Mountfort and her frail gentility until they heard her denounce her son-in-law one morning, enunciating delicately as he took his leave: "You son of a bitch!"

This benighted youth lived on the top floor with his pregnant wife, the Mountforts' older daughter, an offspring even more spectral than her mother, who moved silently in a cold climate of her own, walked without knocking into the lower apartment on vague errands and disdained to answer when greeted. Her husband departed every morning in sergeant's uniform for Governor's Island, stepping out gingerly, sniffing the air, with a scathed look to the nape of his neck, as if he had acquired on the top floor a kind of bewildered mental tiptoe.

The younger daughter, Amanda, however, was a huge blond bouncing girl; she was coming out that winter and she thundered continually down the stairs, taking off from the last step but one and landing with a crash that shook the building. She did volunteer work at an officers' canteen, and late at night Mona and Faith were awakened by the parting of her escorts, British and American— athletic scufflings on the foyer's flagstones and cheery sendoffs over the street. "Call me up!" she shouted blithely. "Page ninety-seven in the Social Register!" Following a large dinner party upstairs, all of Amanda's young men mistakenly burst into the lower apartment in search of bathrooms and had to be herded out, mortified. The Mountforts kept the women below constantly entertained or exasperated or engaged in farcical schemes to outwit them.

The baby, too, unified the household and contributed to its youthfulness. She was now a year old, blue-eyed, not chubby like most babies but looking, as Mona said, "like a very small person in a nightgown," who stood grinning at them over her crib bars. They all loved her, were concerned about her needs, observed her schedule, shared her feedings, enjoyed her droll responses, took a deep interest in her daily advancement. She was a sunny child and never sick, a fact Mr. Mountfort seized upon as proof that cool apartments were healthful.

As the war progressed the apartment became the way station for friends passing through the city, and there were continual welcomes and farewells, impromptu dinners and small cocktail parties.

Then in the second year of the war Clara left for a winter in Florida with Grace and Severance, and Mona, no longer content with her writings, took a Navy job downtown, so secret she couldn't tell what it was she did or where. Sometimes she was on a day shift, sometimes a night, and on weekends she went off to the country to visit family and friends. The apartment was suddenly very quiet.

Every morning of these years Faith awoke with a sense of dark oppression hovering in wait for her: the war. Tony—! Then she encapsulated this anguish, buried it in the night's unconsciousness and rose mechanically to begin the day.

Tony did not write often. Faith was certain this deficiency had to do with his old reluctance to verbalize his feelings for her and the latent, fastidious embarrassment that matrimony caused him. In the first year of the war she had poured out her heart to him in letters, for her own sake as well as his, but his lack of response, his scant, factual V-mail answers, quenched her effusions, and she confined herself to amusing notes. She remembered his reluctance to read personal letters from anyone, especially from people close to him—his mother or father, for instance, when they were abroad; the envelope would lie about for days unopened, until at her remonstrance he would ask, "Read it for me, will you?"

Even his infrequent V-mail letters dwindled. He was permanently stationed in Honolulu and not in danger. He said his duties were very routine and life was pretty dull, but Faith felt there was something conciliatory in this. He never inquired about the baby. How could he forget the child so easily, abandon her from his conscience, all but deny her?

And again, all that was never plainly revealed in their marriage seemed more important, more real than what was evident. Faith could never explain these disparities in Tony—his open-heartedness and his heartlessness, his generosity and the stricture of his feelings, his tenderness and his underlying hostility. Yet without clarifying thought she knew them, she almost understood them. She might have succumbed to the same poisons in herself, were it not for the antidote of the hapless sensitivity to others which produced compassion.

Only when Tony was Mr. Hyde, as she privately called him, the tiger-eyed person he became after one drink too many, did he bring to the surface the terrible blackness in him, a smile of utter cruelty twisting his lips in a sneer.

In this metamorphosis he stunned her one night with the information that both he and Janice were adopted children and did not know who their real parents were.

Soon afterward Janice confirmed this. She had at last broken out of her mother's cage, and she stopped to call on Faith before leaving for London to join her long-time lover. He had never produced a divorce, and indeed there had been times when Faith suspected he was leading Janice on, or even trying to escape her. But for all her mother-domination, her baby voice and china-blue eyes, she had a tenacity, or a need as powerful as tenacity, and a wonderful little pint-sized flame of unquenchable determination. In the last few years, following Mr. Pemberton's death, she had stood up to her mother and hung on to Adrian, her lover. At last Mrs. Pemberton had died, leaving Janice independent and well-to-do, and now Janice was going to live with Adrian willy-nilly.

"Oh yes," she said, of Tony's and her adoption, "it's true. Tony always minded it more than I did, and anyway, Mother forbade us to tell anyone about it when we were little. I guess people were pretty mysterious about adoptions in those days. I hardly ever think about it." She shrugged her sloping Fragonard shoulders. "But it is funny, isn't it, not to know where you came from?"

It explained much: not only physical discrepancies but the schism of Tony's being. He was grateful for his good fortune; his sweetness, his sense of duty, his courtesy were in a sense a demonstration of his gratitude. But he could not in any way be grateful for the loveless void where the meaning of himself should have begun.

Jeff Morrison, a lieutenant commander, stopped at the wartime apartment on his way to Washington, one of the evenings when Mona was home, too. He was already a little tight when he arrived, on the verge of boisterousness, and he tried in vain to persuade one or both of the girls to join him in an evening on the town. They, being sober, had a somewhat subduing effect on him, but his conversation was interspersed with abrupt merrymaking shouts and irrelevant handclaps.

Faith was dismayed. Jeff, the handsome, proud, self-contained youth of her childhood! What had happened to him? She hadn't seen him since Pamela's wedding, when he had come East and she and Tony had briefly chatted with him. He was still handsome, especially in uniform, but under the occupational veneer of suntan his face was gaunt, in some way misshapen, his eyes discolored, glazed, sheepish and evasive. He, too, had been a hero, a cousinly hero whom Faith had respected if not really warmed to. What had become of that marked boyish dignity? He seemed vulgarized, shoddy, counterfeit, as if life had dealt with him unfairly and he had resorted to a continual charade of gaiety. When he raised his glass he winked at Faith: "To Uncle Sam!" and Faith realized he was referring to her grandfather, whose name was Samuel, the one who "drank."

"Oh, hey, I almost forgot," he cried, and snapped his fingers exaggeratedly. "I ran into Tony in the Top of the Mark. Boy, he has it pretty soft, doesn't he—?"

"In San—" A wave, a vibration, of watery coolness washed over her, agitating her bowels. "But he's stationed in Hawaii—"

"Well, official business, ha-ha! Just for a sec, no time to—" He seemed to realize he had put his foot in it, and he tried to pull his face into an expression of gravity. "Y'ah, official business. He was on some mission, some secret mission." He put a finger to his lips. "Very hush-

hush. Matter of fact, we just shook hands, you know how it is . . ." His thoughts wandered, he wagged his head as if in time to some distant rhythm.

Faith, still vibrating, sat quite still, and Mona chatted on, undisturbed. It was perfectly understandable, a mission to the States that Tony couldn't tell Faith about, a drink at the Top of the Mark . . . In a little while Jeff looked at his watch restlessly, said he must move on and took his leave.

But in the night Faith asked the questions that had been lying in wait for her. How could Jeff have known about a secret mission if they had only shaken hands? Tony would never have told Jeff such a thing at a casual meeting in a cocktail lounge. (And would he have gone to a cocktail lounge while on a secret mission?) It wouldn't have been like Tony to invent such a story, either, to put Jeff off. But if he was not on a secret mission, why couldn't he have telephoned Faith? Was this, in fact, the first time Tony had come to the States? Faith moaned and turned violently over in her bed.

There was no escaping it: Jeff was trying to cover up for Tony. Faith remembered his leering. "Boy, he has it pretty soft, doesn't he?" Tony must have had a companion. And Faith pictured a sleek brunette, prototype of Tony's old Vassar girls but now in uniform, an officer in the Waves, large-bosomed, all brass buttons, executive competence and sexual proficiency.

Every afternoon Faith walked Anne in her carriage in the park, the sky pink and gray as the sun receded over the West Side. The wan smell of the wintry city reminded Faith of tea dancing at the Central Park Casino, of the crowded exalted life of St. A. days—the scent of promise, of adventure, all things possible! Anne in her pram grew restless under her mother's brooding silence, and Faith sang to her, pushed her in spurts to make her laugh. She felt acutely the gulf between them—infancy and adulthood, an interval as vast, as helpless as the winter sky, filled with faded colors and lost scents.

Perhaps, she pondered, her mood had nothing to do with the war. Perhaps her sadness was love itself, and even her love for her child was the unbounded giving of what she so meagerly received. She seemed to have reverted to her early Beechwood years, and the more love she gave her child, the more impossible it became to make it up to the love-starved child who had been herself.

When Faith was most childish, most child-ridden, she felt most old. She called out to Tony then, on these bleak walks in the park, needing him, yet knowing it was the old asking, the old need of Beechwood days.

They went home at last for the baby's supper.

And then, the child asleep, the apartment silent, on weekends the entire house empty, Faith sat on the red velvet sofa and drank her sherry alone. Two, or at the most three, glasses, she told herself, although sometimes she was surprised the next day to find the contents of the bottle so reduced.

It was her deliverance. With the first warm permeation, the longing came to an end, and everything contracted into its proper, present-moment perspective. It was like a homecoming, and a glowing immediacy surrounded her comfortingly. She became her own companion and enjoyed her own company. She talked aloud to herself banteringly and waltzed out to the kitchen to start her supper.

This, in fact, was how she wished she could be at all times—droll, wise, forgiving, grateful. True, there was a small pocket of guilt at the bottom of the ritual (drinking alone!), but at the top of it, on what she considered a more rational level, she reminded herself that when Mona was home or there was company, they always had evening drinks. Why not, then, when she most needed them, when they were the only respite from the heart-heavy day? The war! The war could be blamed for everything.

She found she could buy sherry in gallon jugs and not have to count the cost so carefully or run the risk of running out.

The longing for a relative of her own, some infallible relationship, drove her to swallow her pride and telephone her father at his office. Their contacts for a long time had been sketchy, especially since he had sold the town house and bought a farm in Connecticut from which he commuted to Manhattan. Delighted to hear from her, he invited her out for the weekend. When she hung up the phone she gave way to brief, startling fit of weeping.

The farm was set in a rolling stone-walled expanse of fields and woods that in winter had an almost speaking dignity, at once calming and reassuring. And again Faith found herself in her father's environment of quality, except that now it was pastoral and mellower. He had a tenant farmer, and kept a small herd of cows and some poultry, and cultivated the fields. The old house gleamed with polished pine and brass, yet the French and Italian pieces fitted in as well, and opposite a collection of early-nineteenth-century primitives hung one of Faith's first abstractions, an oblong of patched yellows and vermilions.

The atmosphere was warmly emotional, and not alone because of the presence of the prodigal daughter. Perhaps it was the full flowering of the sentiment that had always brought tears so readily to Jack's eyes. (They had filled at once when Faith, carrying Anne, stepped down from the train.) A lavish fire burned in the broad hearth as he mixed martinis, and Violet, wearing a long wool evening skirt, sat quietly knitting and smiling. The fire, the lamplight, the pine and brass, the safety: it was irresistible. And Faith accepted at last the incontrovertible fact that Violet had done wonders for her father, releasing his fervent pent-up capacity for tenderness. Even in his casual catching-up talk, as he stirred the martinis, there was a note of joy. He wasn't particularly interested in Faith's life, and indeed she was well aware that it wasn't particularly interesting, but in his ebullient way he wanted Faith to know all about his own—changes, ideas, wartime contracts, plans for the farm, doings with Violet. Violet, Violet; she shared every moment of his life.

And it was she who took advantage of a pause to ask Faith, "What do you hear from Tony?" Her golden hair was again twined around her head and she wore a pair of blue-framed spectacles on her nose. An aroma of fine soup came through pantry and dining room from the kitchen, where a large country woman was at work, further evidence of Violet's genius, for kitchen help was now almost unobtainable. Faith, going out to prepare Anne's supper, had found the woman incongruously readying such long-vanished niceties as place plates and finger bowls.

It wasn't easy, in this indulgent atmosphere, to prevaricate, but Faith answered, "Oh, he's well!" Her voice was high and bright. "I heard from him"—two months ago? three?—"just recently. He—says it's very dull, if he hadn't had legal training he might have seen some action—well, he's all right, that's the main thing!" She took a quick sip of her drink and lighted a cigarette.

"Do give him our best," said Violet, but Jack, for an instant, glowered. Despite his self-preoccupation he may have sensed something amiss; yet it was more as if he were giving expression to a resentment against Tony of longer standing.

He asked abruptly, "Are you painting, Faith?"

"Oh, yes."

"How is it going?" He seemed already to have guessed the answer.

"Well, not very well. I—there isn't too much time to work, and . . . oh, I don't know . . ." She felt lumpy and drab. "One of Mona's friends, a Norwegian or a Swede or something, who owns a small gallery, offered to show my things if I get enough together—"

"Why, that's wonderful!" Violet exclaimed.

"Yes, but . . . oh, I don't know. The war, and all. My heart just isn't in it." A poor excuse, to her father, who rode the crest of every wave, war or depression, participated in it and was knowledgeable about it, yet stimulated by it; whatever the challenge, it seemed to generate in him in ratio all the more vitality.

He said sharply, "You haven't turned him down, I hope."

"No . . ." The vowel sound ended on a treble note of doubt, and her head drooped.

"You must work, Faith." Her father's voice was gentle now, and urgent. "That's the important thing." He was speaking to her on that other, superlative plane, artist to artist; not chiding or prodding, but rallying her, emboldening. "You have a gift. It's important to you to exercise it. You must be serious about it."

"Yes, you're right." The tone of his voice, so certain of her, addressing a greater worth than she entertained for herself, lifted her in a flood of fresh belief and resolve, and her dreariness sank out of sight like an ungainly walrus. She straightened, her eyes fastening on the painting over Violet's head, and she knew it was worthwhile. It had, now, a vibrant life of its own. She did have a gift (whether great or small was no matter), and it *was* important to her. In some inescapable, ultimate, almost organic way it was even more important to her than the child. She had been puttering moodily with it like a dilettante. Loneliness was good for a painter! "Yes, I've let myself get bogged down." She grinned. "You inspire me!"

He got up and began to replenish the martini pitcher. "Darling," Violet remonstrated, "dinner's almost ready."

"Just one more." He smiled intractably. "We don't have Faith with us very often. We must celebrate." It was his forbearing humor, the one in which Faith had received her first drink. He replenished their glasses and sat down on the sofa beside Violet and took her hand, gazing at Faith. "I never realized," he said, "I was so struck when you and Anne got off the train—how beautiful you are."

Faith might have flushed, shrinking automatically from his doting admiration, but she knew Violet was involved in it too, that Violet in fact was part recipient. Her father seemed free to love her because of Violet, and Faith felt free to accept the remark at face value and be flattered by it.

She didn't think of herself as beautiful, and she tried to see herself in a new way, as her father must have seen her getting off the train—a melancholy face no doubt, large-eyed; the good bone structure revealed by loss of weight. Tony had never once called her beautiful, and with him she never was, never would be. This may have been what her father resented: she took on with Tony a role of almost deliberate self-reduction, shapeless and indistinct, wistful. Whereas here in her father's house, without Tony, with the pair on the sofa, hand in hand, gazing at her fondly, she could be, she was, three-dimensional, someone she scarcely knew except in glimpses, no longer torn between two camps, but one and whole and of substance.

The trouble was, she told herself, she seldom knew what was happening to her, psychically speaking, until after it had stopped happening. Removed from her unlovely, dependent self to this harmonious setting, she could plainly see how she had perpetuated her role of subservience even in Tony's absence. And although her sudden lift of spirits may have been connected with the martinis, still it was a valid alteration and long overdue. Work, to the true and truthful artist, was a transcendence, an elevated level of being which could not be wasted by war, loneliness, marriage or time itself, and she saw her father's selfishness newly as an honorable kind of giving.

She felt like one returning to civilization after a long, grubby camping-out.

The next day was sunny and cold. Jack spent the morning in bed, reading, as he usually did on Saturday, but Violet rummaged about and found woolen caps and mittens for Faith and the baby, and the three of them went outdoors. They were inspired to lower deck chairs into the turquoise-blue bottom of the empty swimming pool, where, sheltered from the wind, the child could safely play and they could take the sun.

Half prone, they began to converse spontaneously, before shyness could set in, on the subject of physical indolence and their predilection for it. Violet knitted and Faith lay with her eyes closed.

"I should warn you though," said Violet, "we take a long walk every Sunday—"

"Oh, I'm used to that. In Beechwood we always did."

"I really don't *like* walking," Violet confessed. "I just

don't like *walks*." Her ingenuousness made Faith laugh. "Up hill and down dale, *smartly*, and my nose runs and my ears ache and I have to go to the bathroom—"

"One's very *bones* get bored—"

"And all the time I'm wishing I were home by the fire—"

"The only place to be on Sunday!"

"Oh, but don't quote me to Jack, please, he'd be terribly hurt. He's so dear, he thinks I don't get out enough. He thinks I need *exercise*." She made her funny giggle, almost a cackle. "He has no idea how much *wild* activity it takes to produce serenity when he gets home from New York."

The conversation was so amicable, and the odd, sensible fact of sitting together in the sunny privacy of the empty swimming pool while Anne played contentedly in its confines, made it impossible not to be communicative. Faith found herself saying, half knowing where it might lead, "Tony makes a religion of exercise, too, only it has to be some form of sport." (Tony's snobbery: taking walks was too middle-class, suburban; even golf was slightly plebeian.) "Tennis or squash or skiing or, if necessary, just plain *running*." She frowned. "*Sweat* is holy." They dissolved in laughter.

"It can't be easy," Violet said, working away at her knitting, "having him away so long. It's two years now, isn't it?"

"Going on three." The need, the overwhelming need, to confide, rose in her, burst. "And I really don't hear from him very often either."

"I'm sure that doesn't help."

Violet's calm response, unsurprised, was more sympathetic than any word of dismay. "I couldn't tell Father last night, I had to lie a little."

"Yes, he'd be furious."

Staring upward at the sky, trusting, Faith began almost inadvertently to talk about her marriage, its sweetness, its vague emptiness, began to tell *someone*, even including herself, realizing from the way the sky looked to her, so unfathomably blue, the sad inscrutable sky of childhood, that she felt much more pain about Tony than she had let herself know. There was a disloyalty in voicing her feelings that was akin to relinquishment, a farewell. She could never again loyally delude herself about her marriage.

And while the revelations came in fits and starts, and Violet's gravely objective comments confirmed Faith's disenchantment, Faith was aware of another sensation, waiting to be recognized, taking place outside the periphery of their talk: a new friendship. Like the turquoise walls of the pool, it rose, surrounded and sheltered the conversation, and Faith never wondered afterward why she had chosen Violet to unburden herself to. It couldn't have been otherwise.

It was time for Anne's lunch, and Violet rolled up her knitting at last. "Both Jack and I suspected all wasn't well. I can't tell you why. Maybe because Tony was so sure of himself and you were not. Faith, I never promise not to tell Jack something, so he'll probably have to know about this, but I won't say anything this weekend."

They got to their feet, and in no time they were laughing again. A purge had taken place. Faith felt light as air. Nothing had been resolved, but it was as if they were both saying, Thank you. Thank you.

Violet had a dinner party that night. Two couples came, sprightly and similar in appearance, and to round out the table, a writer named Conrad Hallam, recently divorced, a shy awkward man who, like herself, Faith suspected, did not readily fit in everywhere, with anyone. He had an affectionate regard for Jack and Violet, and they for him. He was able to interject a few droll words occasionally, and later in the evening he was at ease enough to give vent to a fairly lengthy discourse, free-flowing and scholarly. His books sold reasonably well because of their chunks of near-pornography, but they were heavy going nonetheless, colored with a numbing austerity He was respected but, in a sense, dreaded.

He watched Faith as she watched him, and she fell in love with him and out of love with him in the course of the evening, as if she had run the gamut of an affair with him. His observant gray eyes, his large helpless hands, his silvered hair, his pain and intimated passion, all appealed to her. But as the company moved from library to dining room and back to the living room, she had a presentiment of how these rueful attractions would take their toll of her, and how her own rueful attractions would take their toll of him. Her pulse quickened hopelessly, with the foretaste of havoc, when his eyes moved to her. Love even before it was experienced seemed capable of causing her despair.

Her father was in his element, and the talk was scintillating, but in the back of her mind Faith began to look forward to her comfortable bed and her Agatha Christie novel.

A week later Per Lorngren, who owned the Pontifex Gallery, telephoned her, and she was able to tell him, "Oh, yes, it's going well! I really think I'll have enough to show you next spring."

"You sound as if it's going well. I am happy for you." He had a slight Scandinavian accent which made his words sound blond and cool. "I'm happy for myself. There is a reception at the Modern Museum tomorrow night, they are opening the new Mexican exhibit. Would you like to go?"

"Oh, yes, I would!" She made some calculation. Mona was on her daytime shift and would probably be home to stay with the baby. "Yes, I think I can."

"Good. We will have supper afterward, okay?"

"Okay!"

Perhaps because of her non-affair with Conrad Hallam she was able to be light-hearted with Lorngren. She admired his thin pale good looks uncovetously, felt free to disagree with him and even once or twice good-naturedly mocked his accent. They finished the evening at the Plaza, where they danced. She had developed a reliable and apparently limitless capacity for liquor, never slurring her words or stumbling or getting sick, and Lorngren, too, seemed to have a hollow leg. Under his correctness there appeared a serious Nordic impetuosity, a need to break loose, which she could humor. They drank unnumbered highballs and he got her to smoke a cigar. Before he let her out of the taxi at her door they kissed lightly, half laughing. "You sleep well," he murmured, "and paint well tomorrow, okay?"

"Okay!"

In the hall she was arrested by her whitened vivid face, and paused to look at it. She had to laugh: Was this all it took to relieve the tension of the past two years? Such an innocent evening, and yet this was the glorified face of one who had been love-making!

She found she was hungry for a glimpse of the baby and stole into her room to look at her. At sight of the small skull, turned sideways, the delicate hair, the flushed, hallowed skin, her heart melted when she hadn't known it needed melting, and she felt reprieved from a perilous boredom concerning Anne, and forgiven, and given another chance to love her.

It was this winter that Faith opened the *Herald-Tribune* one morning and read on page three that Janice Pemberton had shot herself in London; she was dead. The top of Faith's skull seemed to lift from her head, and she sagged over paper and breakfast table. In one soundless shout she called out to Janice in protest, in reproach, in commiseration, in farewell. Little Janice going to the opera in a white fur jacket, her hands in white kid gloves folded over a blue beaded bag: little helpless doomed Janice. She had left no notes. Scotland Yard was investigating. Adrian, no doubt, had let her down. The silence of it, the secret sternness— such a merciless, monstrous thing for such a small gentle person to have done! It gave her a stature she hadn't had alive but that had been in waiting to cast its significance over all of her life.

Faith wrote Tony at once, offering what consolation she could, and for several days she listened for the telephone, hoping at least for a cable, and then she waited for a letter. Nothing came.

Late in the winter Claire Gaillard, an old Beechwood acquaintance, called her out of the blue. Claire had been doing USO work and had run across Tony in Hawaii and promised to get in touch with Faith when she was in New York.

She had been a pretty self-contained child, with long golden Mary Pickford curls, whose mother had marshaled her to tap dancing and piano and vocal lessons; it was even suspected that Mrs. Gaillard dyed Claire's hair. Faith had coveted a pair of slippers like Claire's, with six straps buttoning over the ankles, but Mrs. Farrell said they were "common." Since then Faith had followed Claire's career in the newspapers—from the musical comedy stage to Hollywood, not a sensational career but durable.

Obviously she had come a long way from the dainty, dignified child Faith remembered. "My God, darling, I'm scheduled to appear at war-bond rallies or canteens from dawn to midnight. But look, I've got an hour this afternoon, why don't I grab a cab when I finish lunch, as long as you're tied down—for old time's sake, what?"

She came during Anne's nap, late, breathless, flaming-haired, full of cordiality and gusto, brimming over with wartime slang and jokey show-business expressions, erupting with husky "ha-ha's!" She refused a drink in a way that brooked no argument, at once putting Faith off. It would have been a perfect occasion for a friendly drink, even though it was only three o'clock, and Claire's refusal was disappointing and almost like a rebuke. But yes, as a child Claire had been somewhat prim. She perched on the red velvet couch beside Faith and gabbled on and on about her wartime adventures, until at last Faith, with an unintelligible dread, interrupted: "Tell me about Tony."

"Oh, yes, well, we were doing a show out there, you know, and somebody gave us a cocktail party, some admiral or somebody." She switched to the present tense in the new vernacular. "And this glamour boy comes up and introduces himself, and finally through the course of the conversation it dawns on me he is your husband, and we get off in a corner and have a real gas, *howling* about things I remembered about you—don't worry, just silly things about when we were kids—and I promised I'd look you up when I was in New York and give you his love in person. We show people were supposed to go on to a *luau* (my God, I've had ˙˙ with *luaus*), and lo and behold, Tony and his— Tony turns up too, and we squat down beside each other (it's the *squatting* I take a dim view of), and we go right on where we left off. Ha-ha, our dates might as well have been blitzed for all the attention we paid them! But God, he is charming, isn't he—?"

Tony and his date. Claire's exuberance, professional and impervious, set Faith's nerves to quivering, and rage coiled upward in her. "Tell me, Claire," she broke in again, "did *he* ask you to look me up, or was it your idea?"

Claire's eyes widened as she recollected, and then instantly swung away from Faith's face. "Oh well, of course, this was weeks and weeks ago." Her lips pursed and something of her childhood rectitude showed in her face: it wasn't quite decent of Faith to ask this question of someone who didn't practice dishonesty.

Faith relented. "Yes. All right. Never mind. It's just that I suspect he has a mistress."

"So what if he does, darling? Lots of chaps who are stationed overseas for long periods have affairs. It's naïve to think they wouldn't. It doesn't mean anything. It's the war."

There was a ringing silence. Claire went on. "You can't imagine what it's like in Honolulu, Faith, the confusion and all, here today and gone tomorrow, and all those good-looking Red Cross girls. It's like a dream, and the minute the war is over, everybody will wake up and get back to reality."

It was strange, now that she knew: the latent rage was gone. She missed it! The rage must have been due to the mystery, the fact that she alone was to be kept in the dark. Now she felt only an immense cynicism which was worse than rage, more prevalent, more indifferent, in a way

79

more vulgar. There must have been some dignity, after all, in these empty years, some integrity, some hope: the faithful letter writing, the studious following of the news, the scrimping over ration stamps, wearing the Navy pin which she had bought herself, the long, lonely walks with Anne, even the vagrant moments of hilarity; some trust. Here today and gone tomorrow. Ha-ha. He wasn't even in danger! The whole thing seemed demeaningly trivial. Out of sight, out of mind was more like it.

She said calmly, "It's all right, Claire. Forgive me if I embarrassed you."

"Oh God, darling, forgive *me* if I snafued!" She was gathering up her things to depart, returning to her show-business voice, which kept everything aboveboard, generous and simple. The afternoon sun, slanting through the dusty garden windows before it sank behind the rooftops of the houses in the next street, silhouetted her, burning in her fiery hair and glinting in every tiny fur fiber of her red fox collar.

Tonight, Faith thought, I will get drunk. I will get drunk, if I can, all by myself. The thought comforted her.

Her kiss on Claire's pancake make-up was perfunctory. Good-looking Red Cross girls indeed.

She gave in at last and went to bed with Per Lorngren. He had been pleading with her all winter, and one night after a good many drinks she surrendered, but with the same dark cynicism, like a prostitute, not expecting to enjoy it, needing only the intimacy. Vengefully.

After her own Apocalypse she recognized this as the time of transition, when tendencies began to slide into symptoms: the casting about outside herself for someone or something to blame, the rationalizing, the devolution of values, the soul sickness, the soul loneliness, the slow, insidious process of loss.

4

When the war ended and Tony returned she was in the midst of an affair with Per Lorngren.

For a few short months she had been free of shadows. She had begun to realize she was appreciated for herself, that she was in fact appreciable. A flush touched her cheeks, she was always ready with laughter, she gained weight, her hair shone again, she even moved differently. She was productive and had a modestly successful show. She enjoyed the little flurry of publicity and the society of the art world, whose doors, through Per's guidance, opened to her, although to his amusement she was never hoodwinked by its incidental phoniness. She was liked; she was loved.

It was no wonder that she found Tony on his return nearly insufferable. He was embarrassed by her embrace at the airport. Perhaps he dreaded it. He had been in Washington a week before he telephoned her to let her know he was back in the States, and even then it was late at night and she could tell from his voice that he had been drinking; he had needed to be slightly drunk before he could call her. As she ran up to him in the confusion of arriving passengers he removed his white cap and at the last second turned his head, allowing her to kiss his cheek. The week in Washington had evidently been exhausting and his eyes were strangely deadened, but his tanned face was smooth and bland, still bearing an official aplomb from his wartime life.

In the taxi he interrupted his own report of orders and journeys to place a restraining hand over hers and ask her, "Dear, don't, *please*, keep saying 'I see' to everything." His nerves were on edge, as they had never been in the past when his smiling poise carried him through every unpleasantness, and she suddenly felt sorry for him. It was herself, now, she discovered, who was poised, playing the role, not ungenuinely, of warmth and welcome, even of sympathy, safe with her secret of freedom from him.

After Mona had discreetly removed herself for the night, Faith suggested Tony might like to see the sleeping child, now almost four, but he said irritably, "That can wait. Let's go sit down." So they went down to the living room, where in the old way he reluctantly accepted a highball (of precious Scotch which she had hoarded for the occasion!), as if she had suggested something not quite seemly. Then he plunged at once into a full account of his affair with Whitney, the girl in Hawaii. His eyes brightened, and Faith realized he felt gratification rather than guilt in telling her about it. He said it had been a *grande passion*, but in his smile, his volubility—a sort of chatty enthusiasm—she felt a dreadful frivolity. When he had finished she asked him if he wanted to marry Whitney, and he answered at once, "Good God, no!" and told her Whitney was "emotionally unstable" and it was all over. Then, rising, grasping Faith's wrist, his smile the one-sided one he wore before love-making, he drew her upstairs to bed.

In the morning Anne came into the bedroom to meet her father knowingly for the first time, her eyes filled with apprehension and courage, her face white. Faith's heart went out to her. But again Tony was politely embarrassed, propping himself up against his pillows. Faith, unable to witness their awkwardness and thinking they might overcome it better without her, rose and drew Anne forward to Tony's bedside and went downstairs to prepare breakfast.

Her disenchantment was complete.

Tony quickly sensed this. She was no longer hesitant, beclouded. She was no longer dependent. Once more a brilliant indifference in her brought him to heel. He watched her with a kind of lustful surprise and made love to her often. It outraged her that he could forget Whitney and transfer his emotions so easily, so uncontritely to herself.

She got away the following afternoon and fled to Per. He had an apartment over the gallery on Sixtieth Street, and she arrived just at closing time. Per rose quickly from his desk and helped her off with her raincoat and led her upstairs to his living room. She clung to him, gasping half tearfully, aware that her need for him had in the past few days subtly changed to a greater one than his for her, and he soothed her wordlessly, comprehendingly.

"Fix me a drink, darling, for God's sake," she cried. For a little while she stormed up and down the austerely furnished room, gray-lit by the September rain. "He's *trivial*, Per. Isn't that an awful thing to say of anyone? But he is. His feelings are rudimentary and his love is very close to cruelty. Sometimes I think it's a *form* of cruelty. And oh, he said of Anne, 'She's *not* very attractive, is she?'—my

84

beautiful little Anne! And he says these things as if *I* had put *him* in a *rather* unpleasant position and he was *trying* to be good-mannered about it as only a *gentleman* would, to *spare* me! Jesus Christ—!"

"Faith, stop, come and sit down, you have raged enough." His pale eyes shone, and she dropped down beside him. "You are wonderful when you rage, did you know that?" His long fingers had begun their delicious touching. "Your hair turns to fire. It lights up the room." He took away the combs that held it back. "You love *me*, and you have me, and you must not forget how wonderful you are. Turn off the lamp. How nice this gray rainy light is. Poor sweet, poor pet. Yes, cry, I will lick up your tears. Forget him now, forget everyone. Oh, sweetheart, yes, yes . . ."

But already she knew, they both knew, the ending for them approached. An irrevocable shift of atmosphere, paralleling the one from wartime to peacetime, was in the wind. There had never been any question of her divorcing Tony, there was none now. In any case, Per did not believe he could be a husband except to "a simple Scandinavian girl" who would not talk much and would not expect to see much of him except to have three or four blond babies. Now his collectedness, which supervised even his moments of abandon, gave way entirely to tender gravity. When they were conversing quietly he still could not let go of her hand. After that afternoon they were more patient with each other, more passionate, more absent-minded; their detachment from each other had begun in spite of themselves.

Tony said one evening, "Faith, I'm afraid you're going to leave me." He looked like a little boy, gazing at her with anxiety.

She saw her own loneliness in him, and as always, she

was susceptible to it. She would never, in truth, be free of him. For this was the Tony who devastated her, melted all her bitterness, bound her to him. She was committed to him in the marrow of her bones, as she was to Anne. She had taken unto herself his orphanhood, his sweetness, his treachery, and she had not even the wish to leave him. She answered, "No. No, Tony. I'm not going to leave you."

"I love you, Faith, you know that. I do love you." And suddenly he came and knelt by her, his tears falling on her hands.

"Yes. I do know." She put her arm protectively around him and bent to kiss his temple. After all her raging, she couldn't bear for him to humble himself in this way.

He returned to Washington, where he was on temporary duty pending his separation orders. He kissed Faith abstractedly on the cheek, his thoughts already preoccupied with a forthcoming reunion with his old commanding officer. He had been as popular and successful in the Navy as in civilian life.

He never asked her if she had a lover, despite the noticeable change in her. The possibility didn't seem to occur to him or interest him. "He is almost hysterically self-engrossed!" she cried to Per. It was true; she had begun to sense a madness in Tony, or a mad heartlessness. The war had exacerbated the damage already done to him, exploited the innate flaw. His little-boy tears didn't deceive her; they were evidence of his vulnerability, his terrible, untold deprivations: he wept for himself.

It happened that Per had to be in Boston the same week, and Faith drank alone again in her living room. Mona spent most of her time with Shem, who was back in his loft, and they were talking about getting married. Irrationally Faith found herself envious, wishing *she* were getting married, too. She laughed out loud at herself. She drank now prodigiously, without counting the drinks, heedlessly. Her tolerance for alcohol was apparently unlimited, which seemed to her a safety factor: anyone who could hold so much liquor so well could not possibly fall victim to it.

But she had begun to suffer from sleeplessness, and after a fitful night she drank cup after cup of coffee to steady her nerves; then, dressing, she would suddenly go cold and white and have to lie down. She went to see Dr. Farber, a general practitioner, young and zealous, who put her through a series of tests. She drank barium and stood trembling in a muslin gown behind a fluoroscope while Dr. Farber and his nurse exclaimed callously over her digestive system. She sat in the oblivious bustle of a hospital corridor for a good part of a day, drinking sugar and lemon juice and going to the lavatory to give a specimen at intervals.

The upshot of it was that Dr. Farber ordered her to stop drinking coffee in the morning, and to take belladonna and phenobarbital to slow down her rapid digestion.

With these drugs she discovered an easeful, rapturous oblivion. Her prescriptions were renewable, and before long she had abandoned the belladonna and replenished the barbiturate.

Her mother came back from Florida and occupied her old room in the apartment. But the days of wartime camaraderie were over. Mona was seldom at home, and with Per at hand and Tony in the offing, Faith found her mother's presence as oppressive as it had been in Beechwood—more so. She no longer had a place to paint, yet stubbornly she refused Per's suggestion that she borrow or rent a room elsewhere; an awful inertia had come over her and she blamed her mother for it. Her mother's eyelids twitched continuously at Faith's emancipated behavior and abrupt bursts of laughter, and Faith in her turn did not hide her resentment. Soon Clara smelled out her affair with Per, and the quick glares commenced and the disapproving silences. What a morbid talent her mother had for making something reprehensible out of happiness!

But of course it was Faith's drinking that offended Clara the most. She declined to sit down with Faith for sherry, as she had done with Mona. Defiantly Faith made highballs for herself while her mother kept count, she was sure, of her drinks. Often they ate dinner without exchanging a word.

When Faith hinted that Clara might be better off in an apartment of her own her mother uttered her scornful "Hmph!" She had paid her share of the rent throughout her absence and she continued to pay it, and maddeningly she kept her future plans a secret.

It was then that Tony and Clara became friends. He had always had a patient, patronizing attitude toward Clara that mortified Faith, but now when he came up from Washington on weekends and Faith whispered fiercely to him about her mother, he smiled leniently, making her feel childish, and said, "Oh well, dear, never mind, it will all work out." Together, in the living room, Clara and Tony for the first time laughed and conversed at ease, as Clara and Mona had done, and Faith, nursing a drink in her corner, was the outsider.

Yet Clara's return gave Faith more freedom, for Clara was devoted to Anne, and Faith could leave the child in her mother's care. She commenced a strange roaming of the city, to museums and galleries and shops, as if in quest of some elusive exegesis. And what was the riddle? She really didn't know. Was she trying to dramatize something? Even the delayed but imminent parting from Per was not as tragic as she wished it were, and she knew it was not the reason for her floating, almost somnambulistic, wandering. There were times, in the midst of the crowds on Madison Avenue, when she shuddered suddenly with an unidentifiable fear, when for a second or two she forgot where she was going, what her own name was, when the top of her head seemed to float away. She would stop and stare fixedly into a shop window until she recollected herself.

What was happening to her? The winter's well-being had drained imperceptibly away. She felt stranded, at a crossroad.

Yet her fear was disproportionate to her circumstances, which seemed to lack grandeur or consequence. There was nothing, really, to beweep, or believe, or get her teeth into, or feel with all her heart. It was almost as if she suffered from a continual hangover, an oppression that dulled and hollowed her, body and brain. Surely the answer couldn't be as simple, as humiliating as that! Yet the only surcease seemed to come from alcohol, the tender warmth of the evening's first drink, and from its essential counterpart, the phenobarbital.

Pamela Morrison, now Rombauer, briefly roused her, breezing into town from Minneapolis and staying at the Plaza with a good-natured confidence, a quiet affluence. Pamela saw the shows Faith couldn't get tickets for and shopped in the stores Faith couldn't afford, and all without fuss or display, as a matter of course. Faith had seen American women like this abroad and thought what good ambassadors they were—friendly, well dressed, unassuming.

They met for lunch at the hotel. Pamela's mother,

darling May, had died suddenly during the war, and they talked affectionately of her. Her lilting voice, her crooning would live with Faith forever.

They debated ordering a third martini. "Why not?" Faith exclaimed. "This is a special occasion!" Pamela laughed and signaled the waiter, and Faith heard herself gaily adding, "Sometimes I wonder if I'm becoming an alcoholic!"

But Pam answered gravely, shaking her head. "No," she said with unexpected gravity. "No. I *know* an alcoholic, a neighbor of mine. Dan thinks I exaggerate things, but when I stop at her house at ten in the morning, to pick up one of her children or something, she comes to the door reeking of gin. No," she concluded, as if she couldn't allow such a thought, even in jest, about her old friend, "you don't drink in the morning like that."

"No, of course not," Faith answered, relieved. And a little shudder of horror passed over her, as if at a narrow escape. Almost unknowingly she made a vow then, never to drink before noon.

"Well, let's order lunch while we're at it," Pam said. "I've got an appointment at three, unfortunately, so we might as well get going."

Faith experienced a pang of wistfulness for people who had appointments to keep, who had ordered days, however humdrum, and husbands named Dan, or George, or Harry, hovering proprietarily and soberingly over one's life. What if she had married, for instance, someone like Arthur Knox? Would she be content, as content as Pamela? Such people had for her the quality of characters in a soap opera, so homely, so nearly real, so comfortable even in their predicaments, so impossible.

And she noted that envy was becoming habitual with her, envy of the unobtainably prosaic, the elusively substantial. Once more she was aware of not fitting in anywhere, seeking where all her contemporaries had found, adrift, ghostly.

She might have become quite silly and giggly over the third martini, and covertly she watched Pamela for a signal to revert to their old foolishness, the kind, without alcohol, they had indulged in in bygone days, sprawling across Pamela's bed, one setting off the other. But Pamela the matron was not to be shaken out of her offhand, all-governing lucidity. She could be funny but not foolish. Faith realized that after three martinis Pam could still have risen and given an excellent talk to a worthy organization, tallied up a bridge score, remembered the items on her errand list.

It was Faith, the hollow-legged, who contrarily felt fuzzy-headed. With an effort at gravity she inquired after Jeff.

Pam was silent a moment, administering lemon juice to her oysters. She said abruptly, "He's not well, Faith." She looked up and gave the dining room and the stylish crowd around them a blank, speculative stare. "I'm worried about him." Her guileless, troubled eyes came to rest on Faith. "Speaking of alcoholics."

"Oh, dear!"

"Yes. As usual, Dan thinks I'm exaggerating. After all, Jeff is in San Francisco and I'm in Minneapolis. Actually, I can't talk to *any*body about this, except you. God, it's wonderful to have an old pal!"

Faith, reminded of the undecipherable quality in herself that made people confide in her, was flattered, humbled, and felt a flash of gratitude (she counted for something in Pam's sufficiency!), yet the widening of a little stomach hollow indicated her distress. She was about to be the chosen repository for someone's trouble, and she didn't want to be. A curious burgeoning fear shuddered

91

over her. She didn't want to hear about anyone's trouble, even Jeff's! She said, at the top of a stifled, fortifying sigh, "Go ahead, Pam. Tell me about it."

"You know he broke up with his wife."

"He said something about it when he was here."

"And then he was in the hospital a couple of times, naval hospitals, I don't know exactly what with. He said nerves, and that wouldn't be unusual during a war. But he kind of slid over it; he's very evasive about everything. Now I'm beginning to wonder."

She gave her unseeing stare about the room again. "And since his discharge from the Navy he's just drifted about. He only calls sometimes asking for money, and I know from his voice he's not sober and I can tell from the noise in the background that he's calling from some dive or other."

"Oh, Pam." Faith felt the sting of tears, as much for Pam as for Jeff.

"Yes, it's a hell of a thing, isn't it? To think of him wandering around alone like that, broke, in San Francisco. Dan says, 'Oh, he'll settle down, give him time, the war has affected a lot of men this way. Tell him to come on to Minnesota, I'll find him a job.' But I don't know where to locate him, and when he calls I can't pin him down. It's gotten so I don't mention him to Dan any more, and I don't *dare* tell him about the money. I *beg* Jeff to come to us, or let me come out to see him, but he just says, 'Sure, sure, I'll let you know,' or he implies he's got some deal cooking. He stalls me off, and I get nowhere."

She made a grimace. "Well, I didn't mean to cast such a cloud over our lunch, but as I say, you're the only person I can talk to, and it's a relief to get it off my chest. Thanks, pal."

Faith toyed with her consommé. "I don't understand

it, Pam. Jeff was always sort of moody, yes, but he wasn't exactly what you'd call unhappy. He had a happy childhood."

"He didn't lack for love, if that's what counts. I don't understand it either. Such a brilliant mind, and such will power!"

"Yes." Faith could readily summon up a picture of Jeff's youthful expression, his aura of silent self-determination. "In fact, he's the last person I would think would go overboard with drinking."

"Well, I pray for him; that's about all I can do."

She meant it. And Faith imagined Pamela's church in Minneapolis, probably one of the prosperous brand-new structures, all peaked roof and glass, and Pamela emerging from it, neatly attired in suit and hat and gloves, her face composed, unself-conscious. Again Faith felt a twinge of envy.

But she was glad, after all, that Pamela had confided in her. The air had somehow cleared, and not alone because her troubles now seemed small compared to Jeff's. She was suddenly more at ease with Pam. A barrier had been removed. Was it that she, too, had confided the matter of her own drinking? For no note of moral judgment had entered Pam's talk of Jeff, any more than it had entered her account of the woman who drank gin in the morning. In fact, Pamela in the past had sometimes defended Faith against her own self-castigation. Once again she had reassured Faith: she couldn't be an alcoholic.

And when Pam said, "Now I want to hear more about *you*," Faith laughed and answered, "Okay, you asked for it," and told her unreservedly about the war years, Tony's dereliction and her affair with Per.

"But what about your painting?" Pamela interjected, as Jack Farrell had done, as if this were more important

93

than any emotional crisis Faith might experience. Faith found herself brought up short again, adrift and a little resentful. The frightening sense of losing herself cooled her body. Who was this person whose painting people asked about? She envied her, too!

"Because one of the things I came East for," Pamela added, "was to *buy* one of your paintings—with Dan's blessing, incidentally. We've had the house redecorated, and there's a space over the mantel in the library..."

Aunt Grace and Uncle Severance were in town, too, and the following night they all gathered in the apartment. Pamela came, and Tony flew up from Washington. Clara prepared an old-fashioned chicken dinner, with dumplings and hot biscuits and apple pie, and at the end of it Severance leaned back in his chair and delivered himself of a stupendous shout of satisfaction, a ceremonial noise that Grace always shushed but which Severance knew delighted Faith.

"All the little venules and arterials of my portal circulation," he sighed, "are now confronted with an *immense* problem!'

Severance had retired from practice, save for an occasional consultation. Neither he nor Grace appeared to have changed at all, but to Faith's sorrow, they mentioned age and aging. She watched them with an aching fondness, listened to their voices, memorizing them—the way they cleared their throats, coughed, admonished, murmured, laughed. They brought back to her a sense of November, its inexorability, its simplicity, its devotional lament. They accepted decline in a way that made her heart rage with sorrow: No, *stay! Don't* give in!

That night Tony told her he had been approached

about a job in Washington, to set up a new postwar branch of the State Department.

"It won't pay a lot, but that's no object." Tony in fact was a wealthy man, now the only heir to his family's fortune. "The point is, it's an important job and it will be a challenge. I've dreaded going back to the old humdrum firm downtown. But it would mean moving to Washington —that's the only hitch where you're concerned." He looked at her from under his drawn brows. "What do you think, Faith?"

She turned to him, lifting her arms, her face full of amazement. "I think it would be wonderful."

His face, too, broke into an astonished grin. "You do? Do you really?" He met her embrace, throwing his arms around her. "Oh, Faith, I've been so anxious about you, about what you'd say! I'm so glad. I was afraid you wouldn't go."

"It's perfect, it's marvelous." They were both a little tearful.

Saved by the bell, she thought. A *change*: a new house, new surroundings. Away from Per, away from despair. Perhaps even away from the drinking that haunted her. Away from whatever it was that that seemed about to befall her.

"Oh, Tony, I'm so *thankful!*"

5

Dr. Pomeroy had worked out a system that reminded Faith of a comic boudoir routine, whereby his patients entered and exited without setting eyes on each other. (Faith cheated sometimes and looked out the window to watch the foreshortened sufferer emerge on the street below. Was she better-looking than Faith, better dressed, worst of all, more confident?) His quarters were on the second floor of a beet-red Edwardian mansion on R Street, a building converted to doctors' offices, and one waited alone in a shadowy room containing leather chairs and potted plants and copies of *Vogue* and *Holiday*, utterly neutral except for one small oil painting, which in such a setting seemed exaggeratedly original. Voices came faintly from the closed room at the other end of the hall—droning monologues, sometimes a shout of laughter (offensive to the waiting one), often nothing but mysterious silence.

Faith sat staring at the oil painting, an abstraction, ardent yet amateurish, which her eyes knew nauseatingly by heart but which her mind could not remember from one visit to the next. Who had painted it? Why was it there? She set considerable store by a person's taste in paintings; did this purplish, grayish rectangle represent some milestone in Dr. Pomeroy's aesthetic experience? Had his wife painted it? Some obscure anger always stirred in Faith at sight of it. Dr. Pomeroy was one of Washington's leading psychiatrists and sometimes she resented silently this paltry painting, this old house, solid as a mausoleum but so unbeautiful, the lack of an office secretary. The whole setup seemed at times an affront, smugly adequate, offering nothing to interest or reassure, take it or leave it.

Then she would shift in the leather chair and ask herself why her surroundings were so inordinately important to her and she would try to concentrate on *Vogue*. Yet at other times the simplicity was restorative: one was to recognize the room as a way station, not to be enjoyed or become attached to. Its very lack of interest suggested that one should collect one's self and prepare for business.

Click. The outside door softly shut at last on the departing patient, Faith's predecessor, usually female at this hour of midafternoon, her noodle no doubt awhirl with upheavaled memories, doubts, questionable conclusions, elusive glimpses of substrata. The soft fireproofed *click*: how stealthy, secret and solitary!

And now it was Faith's turn, and in sudden near-panic she extinguished her cigarette, put aside *Vogue*, glanced for the last time in her compact mirror, decided whether or not to use the adjoining bathroom. For there was still a wait, five, even ten, minutes of silence, and her exasperation came and went on the heels of piteous entreaty. She glared at her extended paint-spattered sneakers, which daringly she had not changed out of today, and then she got up and paced and turned in the few feet of floor space.

In a rush Dr. Pomeroy burst out of his room and plunged down the hall, clean-shaven, shining, good-natured, fresh as a daisy, said "*Hi*, Faith" confidingly, and at once went to work straightening the magazines and emptying the ashtray (he did actually cultivate the room's anonymity), telling her, "Go right in."

Taking up her jacket and purse, she traversed the hall to the farthest room, its door yawning. It was a place of hushed brown shadows, more plants and more unimposing furniture, everything the same, everything unremembered, a place so ordinary yet so hallowed with prayers and penances. It was the operating room, the citadel over which he, imperviously sane, prevailed—his desk, his phone, his photograph of wife and children, his waiting pad and pencil.

Sometimes in this interval he even took the time to water the goddamn *plants*, chatting, as he moved to and fro, about the weather, the news, or something cheerfully irrelevant, while she sat in the brown chair in the bay window and gazed down at R Street. All her previous preparations—her planned appearance, her planned attitude, the matters she would bring up—fled, trailed out the window, leaving her thin, transparent, her mind a ringing gray space, winking darkly with expletives and particles, all at sea.

At last, sinking into his springy revolving chair, leaning far back, pulling up a trouser leg with one hand and taking up pad and pencil with the other, he brought his attention into focus on her, and smiling, intent, said softly, "Well, now."

Once, in answer, feeling exceptionally confident,

98

pleased with herself, eager to show him how well she could be, she had burst abruptly into tears.

He was middle-aged but youthful. He could smile and look serious at the same time. His gray eyes were kind yet chilling. She loved him at times but did not like him; or she liked him but did not love him. She would not let herself fall in love with him, hungrily and hopelessly as she used to fall in love with unreachable men. Anyway, it would have been hard to fall in love with a man who played golf at the Chevy Chase Club, drove a station wagon, had four children, went to the opera. One of his daughters was in Anne's class at school. She tried, too, to keep him out of the category of *father*, which might have introduced an element even more perilous. He was a *friend*, aloof yet partial; at least, so she wished him to be; and so she wished to be to him.

To his "Well, now," she answered, "Oh, I—" and stopped.

The old motif: Oh, I. Even she could get sick of it. So self-minimizingly unhumble!

She propped an ankle over her knee. She was wearing narrow black slacks over black tights and leotard. Usually she dressed carefully and fashionably, and just slightly alluringly, for Dr. Pomeroy, and if she were going on to the dance studio she carried her tights and leotard in a canvas bag; but today she had left her easel in a hurry (in painting alone she could lose track of time) and she thought perhaps the old sneakers and slacks might after all give her confidence, a what-do-I-care attitude, and she was not unaware that she looked slim and competent.

"I've been working. I'm always spent, after working." At once that sounded self-important—did it not? And perhaps vaguely insulting. But the reaction that came back to her from impervious Dr. Pomeroy seemed merely inert, and rather cozy.

He asked, "How's it going?"

"Oh, good." The thin introductory voice gradually picked up conviction. "I'm still on the new tack. I don't know where it will take me, or whether I'll get enough out of it for the new show, but, oh God, it's so"—she squeezed a fist—"so engrossing! When I paint, I *am*." She caught her breath: Arrogant again? No, true, true!

"Yes." Without taking his eyes off her, he scribbled a note. He said, "And you would be a hell of a lot sicker without it."

"Boy, would I." She thought a moment. Rather, thoughts churned in her brain and she selected one. "Per used to say I would kill myself without it."

Dr. Pomeroy nodded, which didn't necessarily mean he agreed. In fact, his eyes looked sharply remote for an instant, as if he were thinking: Per had a hell of a nerve.

She continued, "Maybe that's why Janice shot herself. She had nothing to—she had nothing that was her life's blood, no sacred responsibility *thrust* upon her, like it or not. Do I sound pretentious?"

"Now what made you ask me that?"

He did pounce; one never trod on firm ground. "Well, I thought I sounded a little patronizing of Janice and I didn't mean to."

He reminded her, "You said 'pretentious' first."

"Oh well, I meant about my work. 'Sacred responsibility'!"

"Faith," he said, twitching again at his trouser leg, leaning so far back in the swivel chair that his feet lifted from the floor, "why are you afraid to talk proudly of your work? A show in New York, sales, another show to come in Washington? It *is* a sacred responsibility, God's gift—yes, thrust upon you, or better, bestowed. I think you are proud of it; at any rate, you know it's good. It *is* goodness, goodness in you. Now why be apologetic about it?"

He was no more hesitant about uttering the word *God* to her than a four-letter word. She bent over, rubbing her forehead with both hands, and this, too, was a phase in the interview. "Yes, I'm being phony about it."

"Now, Faith, I didn't say that."

Oh Jesus, anyone less patient would have given up on her! Was there no end to her wormishness? But now she had reached an impasse, another phase, her thoughts churning centrifugally into a blur, and she was mute.

"Tony?" he suggested softly, to set the ball rolling again.

"Oh, he's very busy. I don't see much of him. These State Department men don't seem to keep any hours. They're—they're like *priests*. They go from morning to night. They have a *gleam* in their eyes. They *know* everything. You tell one of them something that you read in *The New York Times* and he looks at you from a vast distance and says, 'That's not what Dulles told *me*.' Cripes, they're hard to take."

She looked up, her hair falling over her face, and Dr. Pomeroy was laughing.

She said, "We had—intercourse last night." She never could word it easily, it always came out sounding gingerly and a little obscene; even one of Dr. Pomeroy's four-letter words would have sounded less offensive.

"How was it?"

"Lousy."

"Why?"

What did he mean *why*? Because it—she said it out loud, "Because it's like punishment, it's hostile, as if he's saying, 'I'm going to *do* this to you.' With Per it was natural, it got to be natural, a natural thing at the end of a happy evening. It was like exploring, like going into some exotic country together. And oh, I don't know, he's—Tony, he's gotten so *damn* stuffy, so exalted, and when we do talk to each other he all but *pats* me on the head. And in public, at parties and things, when I have the temerity to open my mouth and say something, he freezes me with the most paralyzing stare—" Her voice had been getting louder and louder and she hated the sound of it, harsh, complaining, but disgustedly she persisted. "And of course he wants to keep it dark that I paint, and as for *modern dance*—well, that *really* would disgrace him! So when he comes at me with that crooked little smile and fumbles with those *cool* hands—" She was making faces at Dr. Pomeroy, and realizing it, she heard her voice toppling into laughter, and then she bent her head again with a groan, her arms and shoulders huddled over her lap.

Dr. Pomeroy never hesitated to interpret or express an opinion. "He has conflicts of his own which he has never resolved. In some ways you are evidently a threat to him. He can't recognize you as a person in your own right. You would need considerable charity to go to bed happily with him."

"He *kills* charity in me!"

Dr. Pomeroy nodded again, unconvinced. They were quiet. She said unpremeditatedly, "I had a letter from Mother this morning." He waited. Her voice clouded. "She sounds well but her handwriting is shaky. I don't like that." Tears suddenly hovered in the offing, and quickly Faith got onto safer ground. "I'm glad she's with my aunt and uncle. Florida agrees with them." She put on a specious smile, bored with her own prevaricating.

Dr. Pomeroy was scribbling away. He stopped and

studied her. He said, "Let's talk some more about your mother."

His insistence made her feel a pang of nausea, perhaps because she had already given vent to so much resentment, or because she had given vent to some of it but not all of it. Her voice came muffled from her bowed chest. "What do you want to know?"

"Anything that comes to mind. Anything at all."

"I feel awfully depressed, all of a sudden."

He was quiet.

"At least for once we're not talking about my father!"

Not a word or motion from Dr. Pomeroy. Moments passed. They had come to a crucial unfixed point where time stopped, or time was part of the uncertainty, and she couldn't think. "I just feel very sad."

The silent ticking of time standing still. He murmured, "Tony, your mother, your father . . ."

A great reservoir of unshed tears swelled in her. All the gray sadness of childhood, the bleak skies of childhood, of November, hung irrevocably over her. Supplicatingly her hands cupped her brow, her palms covering her eyes. "I loved them," she offered in desperation, "and they couldn't love me."

He amended, "They couldn't love you the way you wanted to be loved."

"All right, that's probably nearer the truth. And I made them make me not love myself." She peered at him. "Does that make any sense?"

He smiled faintly. "Yes, it does."

"Maybe this is my own unresolved conflict. It feels like a void that's never been filled up."

"Faith, they had conflicts too, remember. I think if you could let yourself, you'd see they did love you in their own way."

"Yes. They must have." The tears began to fall. She reached for the Kleenex. "But it seems so much harder to accept now than it did then!" She shook her head; she couldn't explain herself. She blotted her cheeks. "I hope someday I'll be able to look back on this and laugh. At least, look back on it with pity."

"I hope so too."

"I mean, know how to love myself, and feel pity for this weepy person."

"I hope so . . . Faith, you're a sweet girl."

She couldn't, wouldn't, accept that. She would dissolve altogether, fall into a sickening, fatal well. It was safer to huddle in a miserable heap or shout resentment. She said, "I remind myself of the Rhine maidens wailing, *Wehe! Wehe!* Woe! Woe!" She flung back her head. "Dr. Pomeroy, *what* is the matter with me? What is happening? Why am I worse instead of better? Sometimes I feel diseased, as if I have an insidious allergy, as if I were becoming more and more allergic to life, to myself! What ails me? I mean, if you had to write a diagnosis down on a chart, what would you say?"

His eyes, deliberating, shifted sideways. But he must have decided not to equivocate. "That you suffer from a psychoneurotic depression," he told her, "at times severe."

"Oh." Yes, it sounded recondite enough, yet reasonably accurate; there was even some relief in hearing it.

"Faith, what about the Seconal?"

She stirred in her chair. A pretense of artlessness: "How do you mean?"

"Are you still taking them?"

"Well, yes. Not very many."

"How many?"

The brown-shadowed room looked momentarily fragmented, cross-hatched, as she lied to him: "Oh, only one or two a night." Actually, she didn't know how many, she always lost count.

"And the booze?"

Booze—odious word! But her vision cleared with the truth. "No, nothing. It's been over six months now."

Pamela had written that Jeff had joined Alcoholics Anonymous. It seemed to Faith a squalid kind of moral suicide. Surely one needn't go to such extremes! At about the same time she had had a frightening experience: after one or two fortifying "dressing drinks" she had gone with Tony to a grand dinner party and afterward not remembered anything about it. Nothing untoward, evidently, had happened, for she cautiously sounded Tony out about it the next day, but the total absence of recollection horrified her, opening suddenly the ominous abyss which most of the time she managed to by-pass. (She had had former lapses but they had seemed negligible, of shorter duration, and the occasions unimportant.) It was at the time of her beginning sessions with Dr. Pomeroy, and with something of the old unsparing stoicism she decided to try a regime of austerity and go on the wagon for a while, giving up the one thing she could depend on to fortify and comfort her, and, more pertinent now, to change her.

"I'm much more concerned about the Seconal," Dr. Pomeroy said. "I'd like to see you get off it altogether."

"But I have to get some sleep, Dr. Pomeroy—otherwise I'd go out of my mind!"

"You know it has a cumulative depressing effect."

"Yes." He had told her this before. She sighed. "I have tried. I will try."

He had set aside his pad and pencil and she knew the hour was over, although she was pretty sure they hadn't used up the full fifty minutes. He never hurried her, but she would do anything rather than appear to be hanging on.

She got to her feet, sliding into her jacket quickly so that he wouldn't think she wanted him to help her, and moved to the door.

"How's Anne?" he asked, following to show her out.

"She's fine. The pony came. She's in seventh heaven." But she could tell, even though he was behind her, that he was thinking of something else, or there was something he didn't quite agree with. She stepped aside to let him open the door. "Goodbye. I'll see you Thursday. And thank you." She never forgot her manners.

"Faith, you don't need to thank me."

A rebuff? Lord, she was like some plantlike sea animal, tentacles forever reaching and recoiling. "Well—okay. Goodbye!"

He let her out. Someone else was waiting; she heard a nervous, lamblike cough. Faith, now, was the envied one. The door made its soft *click* behind her.

The outer hall always seemed darker when she left than when she came in. Probably it actually was, since the autumn afternoon had waned and the light had ceased to penetrate the stained-glass window on the landing. But she felt this darkening had to do, too, with leaving the place where anything was possible, the operating room, the opportunity room, the safe omniscience of her wise and patient friend, and having to begin again being the person she grew more and more tired of being—assume again the murky cloak of her own inescapable self. It took all her concentration to get down the stairs without stumbling.

She drove across Q Street to Georgetown and found a parking space and left the car to hurry along the brick leaf-strewn sidewalks, past the little Georgian houses and the police station and across Wisconsin Avenue to the dance studio.

The leaves, the sour sunset-smell of trees and grass in autumn! It was a village-smell, recalling Beechwood. *Wehe! Wehe!* Passers-by glanced at her costume curiously, for in the early fifties it wasn't usual for a woman to appear on the street in such attire, but the private travail of the previous hour inured her from embarrassment.

She climbed the stairs to the studio and the growing tumult of drum and piano and Geneva's voice, cultivated but powerful: "A run-run-*leap*, a run-run-*leap*, come on, Becky—Marcia, GO!—a run-run-*leap*—!" BOM-BOM-BOOM! And large chords pealed from the piano, "Good, Jennifer, goo-ood . . . *girl!* A run-run-*leap*—!"

Unconsciously Faith always broke into a broad grin as she reached the top step, coming upon this pandemonium—flying bodies, thumping bare feet, drum, voice, piano, all in brilliant light, the excitement and innocence of it. Downstairs in the grocery store the manager claimed these climactic leaps made the grapefruit roll off the stand. It was the last of the children's classes, and they came hurtling off the long dance floor and charged for the dressing room, flat-chested, stomachs sticking out, soft heels pounding, hair flying, elbows fending.

Then drum and piano suddenly ceased, giving way to shouts and squeals and a rustle among the waiting mothers as they got to their feet. Geneva, in purple tights and purple velvet tunic, was at once surrounded, and she gave her attention to each person in turn, child or woman, peering into their eyes, her fine profile thrust forward, never forgetting a name, now and then letting loose a fountain of laughter. Addressing Madame Môal, wife of a Belgian Embassy official, she spoke a French almost more fastidious and idiomatic than Madame Môal's own. She had white hair cut in a Dutch bob, a small muscular body and beautiful small feet permanently turned out, for she had once been in the other camp, the ballet, before renouncing it for modern dance.

It amused Faith that Tony, who unconsciously had to place everyone either on or off his own social stratum, could not classify Geneva. She had had almost no formal schooling; her cultivated speech must have been acquired naturally from her New England background and the dusty studios and backstages of Paris and Nice and London, and she perpetrated marvelous malapropisms ("That really got his gander up!"). Yet there was a sensitive erudition, a sophistication, about her person that showed itself even in her fingertips, which none of Tony's admired Vassar girls (now wives of State Department men) could match. Powerful in her authority, feminine in her delicacy and exquisite manners, Geneva baffled Tony, defying his standards, and when she dropped in at the house on a Sunday afternoon, he couldn't decide whether to stay, fascinated, or leave, disadvantaged. Young Anne, who was eight by this time, said thoughtfully, "She's not a person, Mummy, she's a personage."

Faith shed her slacks and sneakers and gravitated toward Beatrice at the upright piano. Faith's hands and feet were cold, but Beatrice glowed like a fire, lanky, crop-haired, chocolate-brown. "Fine, fine!" she cried, in answer to Faith's inquiry. "I gotta be!" She stamped her foot, ducking her head and shaking it like a horse, whinnying with laughter. Faith knew that Beatrice had a hard time making ends meet, alone, with children to raise, keeping meager musical dates all over town. She could play anything with her burning, gallant energy—jazz in night clubs, Bach in churches. "I gotta be!" It was true, she was never sick. Faith would not have changed places with the gangling black woman (the still-segregated "Negress" of the early fifties), but she approached her as if to warm herself, knowing Beatrice's place was more radiant than her own.

Geneva joined them, having disposed of the mothers, sighing "Oh my" philosophically, which made Faith chuckle. "Faith, Faith, how are you?" A warm hug, the childlike dance-world hug, with the cheek and temple and soft white hair pressed to one's own, and then the searching face peering close. Geneva had a habit of reading a person's eyes, divining the lurking shadows of distress or fatigue, frowning at pretense, pouncing on humor. "You're tense," she pronounced at once. "It will do you good to get a workout. Loosen up your muscles. Get the blood circulating." (How simple! Have a workout, get the blood to circulating, and your problems were solved! Was she Dr. Pomeroy's opposite, or his counterpart?) "Did you see Jennifer do those leaps? Such abandon, such *élan!* It may not be dancing, but I like it!" Her great Ha-ha-ha bubbled up, and Beatrice hooted and stamped her foot, and Faith, laughing as much at them as with them, completed the chorus.

Why was it so funny, the way Geneva insisted "I *like* it"? But this was a place of much comedy, where the outer quirks—mannerisms, words—were to be enjoyed, and the inner ones, the weighted ones, were exorcised in movement. Faith had happened to be present when Jennifer's mother first brought her to the studio—dragged her, the child shrinking back. Faith had watched Geneva take Jennifer strongly by the hand and lead her to the circle of children on the floor and begin to coax and drum and erupt now and then with Ha-ha-ha. She saw Jennifer begin to come forward within her own skin, leaving herself and losing herself in the delight of becoming a tree, rain, grass, while Beatrice dramatized on the piano; saw the child fall in love with the flight of mind into motion.

Now the mothers and children had departed and the advanced class was assembling. Besides Faith there were four or five adults, but the class consisted of teen-agers for the most part, their long hair rendered shining and their skin fine-veined by the tone of their powerful bodies. At rest in tights and leotards, they looked meek, nondescript and bulging; but on the dance floor their bodies became fluid, and their faces stately and ageless.

Beatrice rippled out a reveille on the piano. She had to keep track of the hour, for Geneva had no sense of time at all. After the class Beatrice would vanish like lightning for another engagement. Geneva broke off her conversation, put aside her cigarette in a filtered holder, clapped her hands. "All right, girls! To the *barre!*" (She pronounced it *bah*.) She seated herself in her chair on the edge of the dance floor, crouched forward, drum between her knees, and the class ranged itself along the walls in preparation for the long warm-up sequence. Arms were extended in working position. Beatrice leaned over the keyboard, hands poised.

There was a moment of consecration. No one smiled. No one spoke. No one moved.

"*And*—!" said Geneva softly, urgently, and made a grace-noted *puh*-BOM on the drum, while on the BOM Beatrice plunged into the exhilarating accompaniment which she had composed.

After the class Geneva invited Faith to "come in back," as she often did, for a cup of tea and a brief visit. "In back" meant Geneva's living quarters behind the dance floor, a vaguely partitioned area, warm with lamps and soft chairs and filled with mementos—posters of bygone dance recitals, photographs of dancers (including some of Geneva in her youth, draped in chiffon, her long golden hair flowing down her back), framed complimentary letters from the President of France, the Queen of Spain, as well as paintings, caricatures, books on the dance, records, percussion instruments.

And here congregated Geneva's friends, drifting in and out as Shem's friends drifted in and out of his loft—young dancers, joyous or troubled, their souls so untried in their educated bodies, musicians, organizers of precarious high-minded theater groups, picturesque older cronies from the cities of Europe, all prattling away in various accents and languages. Here one memorable evening the godmother of modern dance, beautiful in age, her skin transparent as a saint's, majestic, poetic still in every pose of neck and hands and torso, had held court.

"Geneva, I can't, I've got to rush home and change. I'm meeting Tony at a reception."

"Ah, too bad." Geneva studied Faith ruefully; these receptions and dinner parties were a condition of Washington life for whose obligants she felt only the greatest commiseration. What she didn't ask, but which Faith could see being asked in her steady gaze, was whether Faith were not betraying herself in complying. "You should have a rest, a hot shower and a rest before you go out; a glass of milk. I noticed tonight how thin you're getting. Are you eating well?"

"Oh yes, I guess so . . ." Faith rubbed the damp hair at the back of her neck.

"Well, I won't keep you." The strong hug. "Au 'voir, ma chère."

"Au 'voir, Geneva." She couldn't use endearments as freely and affectionately as Geneva did, except with Anne and Tony.

111

And Geneva answered, like Dr. Pomeroy, "Don't thank *me*." And added, "It's I who am indebted to you."

"Oh no—"

Geneva laughed. "Oh yes. You bring an elegance to this funny place."

"I?" But again she shrank, as she had with Dr. Pomeroy, from the image of such a person, perhaps from the responsibility of such an image. She said quickly, "Geneva, you don't know how much you give!"

"If I do it's a privilege." How enviable, to be able to respond so simply and directly! Geneva's strong regard for her friends put to shame Faith's diffidence. Her comic laugh erupted again. "Here we go again, Alphonse *et* Gaston. Take care of yourself, darling." She meant this literally; she was incapable of uttering empty civilities. "*A bientôt!*"

Recrossing Wisconsin Avenue, darting through a break in the evening traffic, passing again the police station with its glimpse of neon-lighted bald heads and filing cabinets, retracing her way over the brick walks, Faith felt purged by exertion, awakened rather than fatigued, conscious of moving with a firm free waist and back, the muscles minimizing her weight, her sneakered feet merely providing momentum.

She broke into an easy run, skimming the walks, taking in with eyes and nose and open mouth the lamplit windows, the sickle moon, the settling autumn chill of evening. *I am happy, God,* she informed the scene in silence.

God? She smiled. A Freudian slip? Perhaps she was echoing Dr. Pomeroy; perhaps God *was* Dr. Pomeroy. But for a moment she had been filled with such exquisite tenderness for the graceful evening, for herself even, that she felt impulsively it must include God, as if He were an

Innocence too, a childlike presence not to be left out, a reflected tenderness like the delicate moon.

She found her car and turned homeward.

When she shut off the motor she heard at once the surge of the river, a wide, high uproar, rising into the tree-tops of the steep riverbank, arching overhead like the curved roar in a seashell. It stated; it told you it was there whether you were there or not, that the impetus of your life was immaterial compared to its own vast unending torrent.

She braced herself unconsciously, as always, breaching the threshold of this house, Tony's house. He had found it himself, while Faith and Anne waited in New York, and he had furnished it (he didn't trust Faith's more vivid tastes) with opulent conservative sofas and chairs from Sloane's and thick carpeting, all in grays and blues.

The lamps were lit but the house was still save for the faint burr from the television set upstairs; not a sound from the maid's quarters where Naomi lurked. It was a house where everyone went to his lair.

She made a three-noted whistle and instantly Anne answered. Faith hurried upstairs. "Hi, darling!"

"Hi-i!" sang Anne in her treble voice, her eyes still fastened to the TV screen. She wore her blue school uniform and she was propped up on her bed, her supper tray across her lap. Here was the life of this house, Faith thought, its exorciser. Anne held it together, and Faith, depending on her, grieved for her. She kissed her and inspected the tray: fried chicken, a huge mound of mashed potatoes, overcooked beans, salad.

Anne dragged her eyes from the screen. "How was the class?"

What class? In her concern for the child, Faith forgot things that the child, in her concern for her mother, remembered. "Oh, wonderful! We did the Fourth Position Study." She made a *grand plié* in fourth position, and Anne smiled, admiring. "And Beatrice's music—*tah*-tee, ta-*tah*, *tah, tah, tah*—is like a ballad, something very contemplative. I told her it ought to have words—" Her exuberance with Anne was genuine. Was woe unnatural to her after all? For she suspected she was more her real self with Anne than with anyone else. "How was school?"

A shadow fleeting across the creamy face: "Oh, fine."

"Did you do your homework?"

"Some of it." It seemed to Faith that Anne's burden, the burden of her responsibility in this house, showed in her schoolwork. For her voice always took on this note of anguish, and for a child so perceptive, her grades were poor. "Are you going out?"

"Yes, I have to meet Daddy in town, but we won't be late getting back. Darling, put off the TV when you finish your supper, and finish your homework. *Please.*"

"I will." The high, faint voice; Anne's eyes roved to the screen again.

"And don't let your food get cold. *Eat.*"

"I will."

"I've got to change, I'm late as it is—" But Anne was engrossed again, lost. Faith moved away, away from the child eating alone, drugged with a Western . . . She called back, "Did you ride today?"

But Anne didn't hear her.

Faith stripped for her shower, and then in her bathroom she opened the deep medicine closet and took out the bottle of Scotch.

She stood still, holding it, astonished. She hadn't even been thinking about it, to her knowledge. Yet she had reached for it automatically, as if obeying a post-hypnotic effect or a conditioned reflex. Perspiration broke out over her forehead. It was the bottle she had kept handy for dressing drinks. Since going on the wagon she had never thought to remove it; she had almost forgotten it was there. What possessed her? (Dr. Pomeroy had said, hadn't he, that he would rather she drink than take pills?) She stood gazing at the bottle ruminatively, and the internal make-up of her body moved as though reorganizing; tubes and tendrils quivered, rushing fluids hither and yon, masses lifted and resettled, blood soared, surging against the back of her eyes as if to make her weep.

And again her arm, like that of an automaton, a thin pale arm, reached, putting the bottle unopened back in the closet, and shut the door.

She turned on the hot water in the shower and then the cold, scooped up her hair in a shower cap, and climbed in. *Oh*, her body seemed to exclaim, retrospectively, in protest, in injury, *oh!*

Sometimes at these Washington parties there was one person she could talk to, one person with whom she didn't have to exchange inanities, with whom she felt an isolated welcome, both of them smiling: "*Yes*, you and I—!" Sometimes it was a younger woman, new to this wary society, eager and friendly, or an older woman seated alone on the sidelines, her face carved by experience and her eyes still questing; less often a man, for they were the wariest, but occasionally a shy one turned up, or an awed one, or a homely rough-hewn one from Maine or Montana, who didn't intimidate her and showed a predisposition to like her.

But let her encounter one of Tony's favored matrons,

tall, awkward, earnest, saying "pü-f'ctly mah-v'lous," or an omniscient CIA man, or a politician who divined at once her lack of importance, and she stiffened as she had done in her early days, her face flattened, her intelligence extinguished. ("You feel you have nothing to give," Dr. Pomeroy suggested, which she understood emotionally but not intellectually, and could not act upon. Some clue to herself, some simple explanation, perhaps the very core of herself, eluded her still, and even if Dr. Pomeroy had presented it specifically in words, it would have remained a mystery.) It had been easier to get through these parties, of course, when she was drinking, when the dressing drinks gave her an armor, and the secret comfort gave her a secret refuge.

But tonight, wearing topazes and amber wool which matched her hair, she felt almost the same indifference she had felt that afternoon in paint-spattered sneakers and slacks, a fatalism once removed, perhaps, yet safely removed, from despair. Tony hadn't arrived, of course (lately his increasingly overt exclusion of her made him always late when he was meeting her), but standing in the crush, with her glass of ginger ale, she was content to wait, observing with an obdurate, numb remoteness the groupings and regroupings around her, taking note of the appointments of the elaborate room, eavesdropping on sotto voce conversations, assessing exaggerated greetings.

Then the young man with his back to her turned around, offering a nice, plain, debonair face which went well with his conservative buttoned-down attire. They introduced themselves and got off to a good start, somehow discovering they were both devotees of a local advice-to-the-lovelorn column, and with great enjoyment they discussed recent appeals and recommendations, aware that this was not a likely topic for so prestigious a gathering, and they laughed so much that people turned around to look at them with amusement.

In the midst of this exchange Tony appeared. He had been making his way through the crowd, shaking hands with acquaintances, and he shook hands with Faith, and smiling, moved on, saying, "I must go and talk to Radichek."

His handshake affected her as if he had slapped her; she could feel the shock in her face. It may have been her laughter that put him off, but more likely it was the old embarrassment, the thing that would not let him expose his feelings for her, warning her: Don't claim me! The young man, whose name was Owens, went on blithely chatting, but Faith felt a blood-cooling abandon move over her, which might have been pride or might have been absolute humility.

She seldom looked boldly into another's eyes, but now she looked into Owens', and his kindly expression brightened and expanded. He interrupted himself. "Was that your husband?" he asked, and added with the contagion of her own abandon, "Who greeted you so warmly?"

But the same pride made her defend Tony, or the humility would not allow her to take advantage of Tony's failures. (Perhaps he tested her thus, knowing her loyalty was equal to his defections.) "He is shy sometimes in public."

"Well, here," said Owens, "I am not. At least, not with you." And blushing slightly, he leaned forward and planted a gentle kiss on her cheek. "Hello!"

And coloring also, she answered, "Thank you." His open warm-heartedness, coming on the heels of Tony's coldness, completed her disruption. She was smiling, but the swarming room, the air, Owens' pleasant face, had become dazzling, precarious, and she found it hard to breathe.

He said, "You know, Mrs. Pemberton, we may never run across each other again, and I have a charming wife somewhere in this mob, but I love you."

Panic seized her. In the next moment she might burst into tears, as she had done this afternoon, melt into a crumpled heap. "Yes," she said. And with a kind of distant surprise she heard herself add, "I love you too. I must leave. Goodbye."

He stepped aside. "Goodbye, Mrs. Pemberton." And he watched her go.

She collected her coat and left the building. She drove straight home, went straight upstairs, passing Anne's room, where the television still rasped, entered her bathroom, took out the bottle.

The inevitability of it was the ultimate bitterness: she must have meant all along to do this. Shaken with whispering dry sobs, for loneliness, for defeat, she poured out the drink in the plastic cup, permeated with the putrid smell of past drinks, which she kept in the closet along with the bottle.

Just one, she told herself, pleading, justifying—just one! But of course she knew in her bones, as she had known she was going to drink again, that for her there never had been, never would be, such a thing as one.

It was like returning to the arms of a lover, even a treacherous lover; her husband's coldness drove her. She had postponed it as long as she could bear. Or on the contrary, perhaps it was a leave-taking, a farewell to a most dearly beloved: she saw a little figure alone on a shore, motionless in sorrow, betrayed, abandoned. Tears dripped from her heart like blood as she drew away, for it was herself she relinquished.

She brought the cup to her lips, and with difficulty, forcing the liquid down her constricted throat, she drank.

6

Time in those years was confused or lost entirely. Events were misplaced, nothing could be pieced together. When was it that Geneva came to stay? No verbal arrangement was made. She was simply there, one Sunday morning, downstairs with Dr. Pomeroy, while Faith lay in her bed, her eyes blackened, her pillow bloodstained, her mind wandering in the bleached corridors of bariturate catalepsy; their voices droned on and on in druidic determination of her fate, while Tony, on whom they blamed everything, lay alone outdoors on a chaise on the terrace, staring at the river.

The night before, after the one drink too many that released his savagery, he had told her he'd regretted their marriage from the beginning. This was true, she knew, for his heartless self, yet not for the vulnerable one who wept at the possibility of her leaving him. But lately she had begun to give way to a hatefulness of her own, a bitter, vengeful recklessness which set out to inflict torment on him and which she was well aware invited disaster. His drinking habits were incomprehensible to her. He never craved a drink; he could do without alcohol entirely and apparently never think of it, indeed might never have drunk at home at all had it not been for Faith's inveterate "cocktail hour." But once started, he was apt to lose control. Having had a good deal to drink last night herself she had reached a plateau of poised indifference, and she taunted him as though daring him to perpetrate the assault he had so long restrained. And even while he beat her he apologized breathlessly, "I'm sorry, but I *have* to do this!"

It was then that Geneva came to stay, slept in the bed near Faith's, coaxed food into her, often helped her to and from Dr. Pomeroy's office when she felt too ill to drive herself, and at the same time somehow managed to conduct her classes. When Faith, rousing herself from the descending blackness, the spiritless self-engrossment, turned to her with wonder and expressed her gratitude, Geneva answered sadly, mysteriously, "You are two fine people."

And Faith, vaguely angered, saw them standing shoulder to shoulder, the two fine people, male and female, upright, well dressed, handsome, *nice* people, a pair who might almost have existed, like a perfect couple in a re-membered movie—all but believable.

Sometimes her impotent rage turned even on Geneva.

One afternoon as she went to the liquor closet, Geneva remarked quietly, "I knew you drank a lot, Faith, but I had no idea how you really put it away."

Faith whirled on her. " 'Put it away' indeed! It's no-body's business how much I drink. I'll drink as much as I please and I don't want to hear any remarks about it.

My God, you would drink, too, if you were me." She was nearly sobbing. How could she express it—her need, her helplessness, her dismay? Geneva was staring at her in silence with the same mysterious sadness. Faith put out her hand. "Oh, Geneva, forgive me, forgive me, forgive me."

After that she was more secretive, hiding bottles not only in her bathroom closet but in her studio and in the library bookcase.

She had given up her class at the dance studio. Her thin, toxic body went limp at the *barre*, dissolved in invalid sweat, her feet caved in. She painted little. When she forced herself to work she was sickened by what she produced. The Georgetown show had to be postponed.

She attended few social functions. How perverse she had become! When she was among company she longed to be alone, and when she was alone she longed for company. She received a disconcerting phone call from a friend: "Faith, I just thought I'd better let you know, the dinner party we asked you to was *last* Friday night, not this Friday." Bewildered, Faith protested; she had no recollection of the invitation. The voice laughed. "Oh yes, I asked you on the phone a couple of weeks ago." Faith was sure her friend had made a mistake, but something warned her not to argue the matter. Had the unexplained memory lapses begun again? She thought she detected a quizzical note in the voice. She made her apologies.

Even the ball at the Corcoran Gallery was a disappointment. They went with the same friends year after year, and Faith always loved it—the elegance of the throng, the champagne, the dancing among Greek columns and works of art. But this year she had a sense of isolation akin to her wallflower days. Dressing and putting on make-up, she could not beautify herself: there was something about her skin, her pores, her eyes, a yellowish, swollen look, that defied cosmetics. She willed her face to brighten, and it would not. Usually cautious about her drinking in public, she consumed glass after glass of champagne without caution, yet it had no effect on her ponderousness, and merely dulled her the more.

"I keep feeling I have a disease!" she insisted to Dr. Pomeroy. "As if I've caught something, something like a virus that I can't shake off!"

Once, as if in a token to the truth, she told him she thought she was drinking too much. It slipped out innocuously, minimizingly, more like an offhand report than an admission. She had contrived to make it sound that way, yet she felt compelled for the sake of her own fear-ridden conscience, her own safety, to let him know. If she couldn't mention her drinking to Dr. Pomeroy, it must mean there was something wrong with it.

He answered, not disturbed either, for he rarely showed disturbance at anything, "Yes, I've thought sometimes you'd been drinking before you came in here."

"Yes, I have been, sometimes." How dishonestly honest! For she had begun to have drinks now at noon (no one, still, could accuse her of drinking in the morning; the drinks taken between pills, at three or four A.M., didn't count as morning drinks, since it was nighttime), and she almost never came into his office any more when she had not been drinking. She still held it well; often even Geneva couldn't tell. And the fact that her drinking had increased over the past few years, ever since she had gone off the wagon, she explained as proof of her unlimited capacity.

Thus a part of her brain, without her being entirely aware of it, was constantly at work, weighing, rationalizing, protecting her—even from the ignominy of her need for protection—erecting a wall of reassuring opaqueness, a wall on whose sheltered side she felt preserved from the sense of imminent doom, from total disintegration.

"It seems to be the only thing that holds me together," she continued, to Dr. Pomeroy, "the only thing that saves me from madness. And Geneva says I am a person of tremendous control!"

He answered, "If you didn't have so much control, you wouldn't need to drink." It was one of the cryptic remarks she pondered over after she left his office. "What we have to do," he said, "is try to get rid of your problems at home, and then we can do something about your drinking. Faith, why, why, do you stay there, why don't you leave?"

She kneaded her hands together; she couldn't answer him. How could she leave Tony alone? Or perhaps the answer was, Where could I go?

She took Anne to New York during Anne's spring vacation.

Released from the monotonous landmarks of her days —the gray prison of her house, Dr. Pomeroy's office—and with Anne for company, Faith was suddenly happier. Tony, as always in situations where he could be generous, gave them carte blanche. Jack had reserved for them a suite in the apartment hotel where he and Violet kept a *pied-a-terre*, and they stayed a week. It was fun to guide Anne around the city. They shopped, they had tickets for the Philharmonic and the circus and *My Fair Lady*. They went to the Music Hall and lunched by the fountains at the Metropolitan Museum. Jack and Violet took them to the Stork Club. The hotel kitchenette provided ice and Faith made drinks for herself without guilt: it was a holiday!

Anne shared her mother's gusto with some reserve. One might almost have thought Faith the child and Anne the adult. Anne had always been a refuge in the sea of Faith's own floundering, a stability she had come to depend on for a basis of reality. Now in her early teens, Anne and her affairs, her comings and goings, her antic friends and fledgling admirers, her fads and fashions and endless phone calls, all lent their vitality to Faith. As in the past, Anne kept the house alive.

But lately the girl had become somewhat remote, almost taciturn. Alone with her mother in the hotel, between forays, she retreated into books, answering politely but not looking up when her mother, sitting with her drink, interrupted her. And then one morning Faith heard her make a date over the phone to spend the night with a classmate, one of the school's boarders who lived in Manhattan. She made the date eagerly, unhesitatingly, with quite a different tone of voice, never pausing to consult her mother.

Faith panicked. Alone in the hotel room even for one night, she would fall prey to the looming, unnamable fear. Jack and Violet were entertaining friends and did not invite her to join them. Mona, now married to Shem, lived too far away, in Nyack, and Faith was reluctant to look up one of her sedate St. Anne's friends. She ruled out a solitary evening at the movies. It was raining; it would be a rainy night. There was no TV set in the suite. They were on the twenty-third floor and the height suddenly menaced her.

But Jeff and his new wife had returned to the East,

and on their Christmas card Jeff had written a note: *Call me when you're in town.* As a last resort she dialed his office number.

Uncharacteristically, he expressed genuine pleasure. "When can we get together?"

"Oh, gosh, Jeff, I don't know. As a matter of fact, this is the only evening I have free."

"Well, come on out to Montclair with me, why don't you? I'll call Celina, she'll be delighted. Stay over-night with us and I'll bring you back in the morning." He was authoritative as well as good-humored. So unlike the old constricted Jeff! "I'll pick you up at your hotel at five-thirty."

Anne left in the afternoon and Faith spent the rest of the time wandering to and from the bottle in the kitchenette. The fact that he was purportedly a member of Alcoholics Anonymous didn't deter her; it merely testified to his present strangeness, and by its very incomprehensibility had no bearing on her. In any case, she trusted her ability to disguise her drinking. At loose ends in the empty suite, she couldn't help herself; there was nothing else to do.

Jeff was there on the dot. The doorman hurried her to the car under an umbrella, horns sounded behind them, and there was scarcely time to exchange greetings or get a good look at each other in the semi-dark before they set off through the crowded wet streets. Between pauses, while he maneuvered through traffic, they traded family news. Jeff seemed quite at ease, but Faith wasn't sure about herself. He was changed, yet oddly, not a stranger. He had a new maturity that contradictorily made him seem more youthful, as though he had shed the distortions of moodiness and clownishness to become an intrinsic Jeff, both disarmed and disarming, whom she had never known except by intuition. She hoped in the car's steamy close quarters her breath didn't give her away, and surreptitiously she sucked on a Cloret.

They arrived at last at Jeff's ranch-type house, and his new wife turned out to be a beauty—tall, dark-haired, creamy-skinned, with a placidity which aroused in Faith a vague antagonism. But Jeff made drinks generously, to Faith's relief, never letting her sit for long with an empty glass, although she noted with the same stir of antipathy that Celina took only one drink and then forgot to finish it when she went out to prepare dinner. Jeff drank tomato juice, yet he didn't seem unhappy about it, stretched out comfortably in his leather chair, and Faith's initial uneasiness about his abstinence passed.

When dinner was ready she put aside her glass and got promptly to her feet. This was the guardian part of her brain at work again: the fact that she would rather drink than eat must be concealed. Her aversion to food had become a kind of war within herself, against herself. She was always hungry but she hated eating. Faced with a plate of food, a nauseated glumness descended on her; she resented it, the solid gobs had no taste and she pushed her fork at them contemptuously, scowling like a contrary child.

Nevertheless she put on a good show for Celina and Jeff, tucking food in and chewing it up as best she could, all the while exerting herself to put forth praise, charm, interest, laughter.

It was over dessert that Jeff suddenly said, so casually, so momentously, that Faith for an instant mistrusted her ears, "I'm going to an AA meeting tonight. I thought you might like to go with me, just out of curiosity."

There was a split second while Faith turned to look at him, her ears doing a double-take and a hot explosion warming her chest. She glanced toward Celina, but she was silently waiting for Faith's answer and smiling with her maddening tranquillity.

"Why . . . sure," Faith said at last faintly, getting her breath, perspiration breaking out on her palms and the folds of her arms. What else could she say?

"Just out of curiosity," Jeff reiterated encouragingly.

"Sure, I'll go." She held back a sigh, and then let it go with a laugh, blurting out, "I don't want them to stop my drinking, that's all!"

"Oh no," he assured her. "Of course not." He smiled. "We're not bottle-smashers. I just thought you might be interested."

And Celina, who was no help at all, said, rising, "I'll bring the coffee right away."

Faith sat mute and stunned. There was no way out of it. She had heard somewhere that these AA people were like the Oxford Group, getting to their feet and in a welter of self-abasement volunteering confessions of their shameful lives. Would they make her feel moved to get up, too, or call on her? Well, she would not, she promised herself, she would *not!* And her guardian brain began building a bridge over it, counteracting its possible effect, rescuing her in advance with disdain. She could hear herself telling Geneva, "And my God, what do you think, I actually went to an AA meeting with Jeff—just out of curiosity, of course . . ." It would make amusing dinner-party conversation—in case she was invited to another dinner party. She pictured herself regaling her right-hand partner . . .

The meeting was held in the basement of a church, a heavy early-suburban structure, built about 1915, of stone and timber, overly buttressed. Its basement, paneled and beamed in dark varnished wood, smelled of fifty years of

Bible classes—childrens' rubbers, head colds, chalk. She remembered it well from Beechwood, for although her parents had forsworn religion after an excess of it in their own upbringing, they had sent Faith with Pamela and Jeff to Sunday School.

She hung back a little behind Jeff as they entered the AA meeting, the breath in her body almost driven out by a devastating sense of being an outcast, more degrading than any displacement she had ever felt before, more frightening, even, than entering Dr. Pomeroy's office for the first time.

But a dozen or more quite ordinary-looking people stood about—men one might see waiting for a commuter train and a few housewifely women in sweaters and skirts (could *they* be alcoholics, she wondered, eying them covertly?). No one took particular notice of her, greeting her casually and turning to converse with Jeff, with whom they were evidently well acquainted. They exchanged a good deal of banter, smiling and laughing (were they putting on a show of light-heartedness?) and there was an atmosphere of unchallenging informality.

It was their ordinariness that quieted Faith. They seemed to be people who were incapable of indulging in embarrassing ceremony. She could even feel superior to them: *she* was more elegantly dressed, more sophisticated, more accomplished! She was not one of them. She had never been the type to join hearty, homogeneous groups. (Once Dr. Pomeroy had told her quite kindly, "It may be of some comfort to you, Faith, to know you're not really very different from anyone else." He meant only to be helpful, but she had had to hide her outrage.)

They began to take their places in the rows of folding chairs, and Jeff, seating himself beside Faith, leaned forward intently, as if prepared to give himself up without reservation to the proceedings. At the front of the room, on a platform hung with a banner inscribed, *But for the Grace of God*, a jovial chairman said a few words, audible but meaningless to Faith, and then introduced three visiting speakers, two men and a woman, from Passaic, New Jersey. Thank God. Spontaneous confessions from the audience were not, apparently, the rule.

Afterward Faith didn't remember a great deal of the meeting. She had been drinking most of the day and her memory lapses were now a daily occurrence (she couldn't remember much of *My Fair Lady* either). In any case, her brain as usual screened out all that was too painful, perhaps too pertinent, to hear, and gave entrance to all that was reassuring.

These speakers, unlike the suburbanites in the audience, were much more what she had expected alcoholics to be, indeed hoped they would be. Although clean and neat, they spoke ungrammatical English with lower-middle-class accents. They had false or missing teeth; they had all been in jail at one time or another; they had lost jobs, families, homes. And Faith, who found in them not the slightest relevance to herself or even to her drinking, was comforted by the gulf between them.

She remembered best the woman speaker, whose dyed black hair was elaborately coiffed and who wore matching necklace and earrings of glittering blue stones, which in turn matched the harsh cerulean-blue of her rayon crepe dress. Had she gotten herself dressed up for this occasion? She beamed for joy, showing her false teeth and deepening the lines of ravagement in her face and neck.

She lived over a bar, she told them, chuckling, and everyone chuckled with her, including Jeff, but she declared she was grateful to have a roof over her head, and the bar served to remind her of unhappy yesterdays. Of this sordid past she then proceeded to launch into a care-free account, holding back no sorry detail—commitments to mental hospitals, lock-ups, removal of her children by the state . . . Her voice faded as Faith, shuddering, lost herself in a dreary picture of the woman's parlor ceiling, aglow with the red and green neon lights of the bar below, the accumu-lated smells in the downstairs entry, the late-night shouts and scufflings, the awful silence at four in the morning.

Yet Jeff still crouched forward, giving the woman his fullest attention, as if her squalid testimony contained for him some significance of the greatest value: this proud, in-telligent man, hanging on the words of a beaming, battered woman from Passaic! And Faith observed the same sur-render of attention in the other men and women around her and was appalled by it. The chairman had asserted at the beginning of the meeting that AA was not a religious organization, which was a relief to her, but she felt a religiosity in the total affirmation of these listeners, an almost tangible humility, an abhorrent wholesomeness.

"I've been sober four years," proclaimed the woman, "and life is so wonderful . . . !"

Oh God, Faith thought, no. She had despair enough in her life without being caught up in something like this. Save me from this! From such pathetic optimism, such abysmal simplicity, such acceptance of disaster! She longed for the meeting to end.

There was nothing, she thought defiantly, that would cure her revulsion but a drink.

They rose at last to recite the Lord's Prayer. Jeff, too; Jeff bowing his head. And then, as the voices chorused the words, not mumbling them but uttering them dis-tinctly, declaring them, something within her, something like a little silver fish of receptivity, escaped her and slipped, slithered to the surface, put its nose out for a salutory breath as fishes do for oxygen—the lifegiving breath from a deadly atmosphere, and for one instant she joined the others in prayer, thinking, feeling, Yes, yes, it's good. It is good, it is goodness. And then, the renegade minnow of herself sinking down again. It is good for *them.*

The meeting was over.

They went home. One or two men from the meeting followed Jeff for coffee, and there was a bustle in the kitchen. Celina had retired to bed; what self-possession! Jeff turned to Faith where she stood to one side in glum desperation. "What will you have, Faith?"

The answer pushed out: "I would like a drink!"

A faint smile quirked his face but he answered without a second's hesitation: "Scotch or bourbon?"

Faith and Anne returned to the gray house on the river bluff. Tony was glad to see them and as a rare tribute got home in time to have dinner with them. But the next day the house emptied, and Faith, waiting with a vodka and tonic for her appointment with Dr. Pomeroy, realized nothing had changed. She was back in the same trap. It seemed to her a house of deepening sickness, as if the morbidity existed contagiously within its walls, and she was its victim. *Oekophobia,* Dr. Pomeroy called it.

That night Anne announced she desired to become a boarder at the school where she was a day pupil.

Faith couldn't believe she was serious. She stared at the tight, closed face and saw the teen-aged Anne for the first time as separate from herself. Sharing the child's life had meant everything to her! But Anne could not be dissuaded; she insisted Faith go and see her headmistress.

What an interview! Miss Mountfort, seated behind her desk like a deity, disdaining to look at Faith, and Faith wan, fibrous in her morning shattered state between her last pill and her first drink (this was the calculating part of her brain at work again: she could drink before an appointment with unshockable Dr. Pomeroy, but not before one with Miss Mountfort), trying to persuade this haughty, brainy spinster to consent to something that would break her own heart!

"And anyway," Miss Mountfort concluded, after enumerating various deterrents, "why should she want to come in as a boarder? She has a happy home, hasn't she?"

Cruel bitch! Oh yes, Faith told her, oh yes, of course, with a widening horror in her mind, her lungs. Was it so terrible, then, for Anne, the home of those two fake-fine people—so unbearable? Was she escaping the nameless sickness of the house? Even Naomi, the maid, had left—fled, almost.

And the upshot of the interview was that Faith was refused, the school's beds were full, and she went away reprieved, numbly thankful.

But Anne took matters at once into her own hands. She looked bruised, hearing her mother's report, the skin under her eyes and cheekbones darkened. Stubbornly she said, "I'll talk to her myself."

It took only a short time, it was over very quickly. Anne was packing her things. Faith couldn't believe what was happening. "Couldn't you wait until Monday? Couldn't you just stay the weekend?" And silently she was crying, again as if she were the child and Anne the mother, Don't leave me, don't leave me!

She could never let herself imagine what Anne must have told Miss Mountfort to make her change her mind.

She began then not to care. The controls she had exerted weakened. She took enough Seconal to render herself unconscious until noon, and she poured her first drink on arising. She felt she was approaching the brink of the abyss.

"I'm afraid, Dr. Pomeroy, I'm afraid. I'm afraid I may kill myself."

7

6B was the psychiatric ward of the university hospital where Dr. Pomeroy lectured—not a very large ward, for as far as Faith could tell, it was for people needing emergency or short-term treatment, like herself. It comprised a few private and perhaps a dozen semi-private rooms, and there were seldom more than thirty patients, both men and women. Nevertheless they were confined, and the elevator doors were securely locked.

Away from it, Faith thought of it as a limbo, its clean oatmeal-colored walls lighted with the sorrowing rays of the sun setting over Washington, filtered through extra-heavy screens, or the silver of a rainy Sunday morning. It was a place suspended on the fourth floor in the middle of the city like an event in a dream, without a beginning or an end, irrelevant yet heavy with meaning. The patients themselves were neuter, only vaguely male or female, the men in loose pajamas and robes, with their rooster necks pathetically exposed: the women shapeless, childish, defunctionalized in pretty negligees.

Shock treatment was still extensively given, and every morning Faith (on whom Dr. Pomeroy was trying the new tranquilizers) cowered in her room as the protesting patients were rounded up and led wailing away to the treatment center at the end of the hall. Later in the solarium she would console them as, dazed and nauseated, they huddled with their heads in their hands, groaning softly, trying to remember their names, querying timorously, "Did I tell you if I was married? Do I have a family?" Recalling in her own home this routine little morning commotion, the howls and wails, the kindly wise-cracking insistence of the nurses, Faith would shudder. It was hard to believe something so barbaric was happening so casually every day in the heart of the city. She had never actually witnessed the scene except with her ears, but she pictured it as drawn by Hogarth, with contorted figures done in ominous ochers and siennas.

Yet each time Dr. Pomeroy sent her here, she got better. Once within the ward's locked doors, she accepted its isolation gratefully. Even the suspension of her drinking was tolerable. Here it was possible to give up the daily, nightly struggle of her real world and lapse into a kind of syncope of dissociation.

She could no longer keep abreast of her ordeal; its tenacity, its progression exhausted her. But here in 6B its burden merged with the pooled ordeals of all the other patients, and relieved of its weight, she listened with curiosity, almost insatiability, to the ruminations, the complaints and hopes, of her fellows. No one said why they were there and no one ever asked. Faith searched, fascinated, behind their apparent normality for a clue. She

135

pieced together their lives and contrived mental pictures of their homes and families. She felt for them an unequivocal compassion. No matter how forbidding or unlovely or remote they might be, she cherished an all-embracing favoritism for them.

Yet this compassion was limited, too, to this place; she could put Tony entirely out of her mind, she could even forget about Anne for long periods.

6B came to seem, in fact, a theater more absorbing, more dramatic, more poignant, than any arena of her real world. Indeed, when she was there, safely locked in, it seemed more real than the real world, as if in this ward she was privileged to behold the underlying truth of all reality.

She felt a terrible peace in 6B, a costly mercy, a thankfulness only a gate away from the flood of tears she had never unloosed. The tremors of her hands subsided, her face improved; a blooming inner clarity blanched the skin, tightening it. The hideously writhing designs behind her pupils receded. She made herself useful; she was liked by nurses and attendants. She asked for materials from the OT girl and drew charcoal portraits of her fellow patients, and there was a benefit in this for both artist and sitter. How marvelous the indentation of an eyelid, the curve of an upper lip! With a tenderness new to herself, she found beauty in the most ordinary, depreciated face. While she worked she shared her observations with the sitter, and it was part of her reward to see the face take on a moving, modest wonder at its own distinction.

Dr. Pomeroy, dropping in on her, smiled at her with gratification. They sat in her room, she with her robe carefully drawn across her lap, and talked about Pasternak and baseball, avoiding by common consent her troubles. There was a pleasant warmth, slightly sexual, in these meetings. He would rise and touch her knee in farewell. They had an agreement: she let him admit her whenever thoughts of suicide possessed her.

After a week, ten days perhaps, she would go back to the gray house.

This time Geneva came to take her home, imperiously scooping up her books and suitcase, setting the attendants to laughing. With her snow-white hair, her distinguished profile and voice, her swaggering toed-out walk, her innocent obliviousness, she always attracted people: who was she? One wanted to know her, not so much because she was so obviously a personage, but because she so obviously possessed some key to life-enrichment, some resolute, slightly comical, unabashed validity.

And wherever Geneva went, to a concert or the supermarket or even a hospital, a pupil or a former pupil or the relative of a pupil would call out, and she would pause to exchange news and laughter, her head attentively inclined forward in a European way, making in the midst of traffic a joyous little conclave. Afterward she would elucidate gravely to Faith, "I taught her when I had the old studio on Connecticut Avenue, and now she's grown up and has children of her own. Oh my! A charming girl, but she had such trouble putting one foot in front of the other . . ." And Faith would explode with laughter.

Once Geneva confided, "When I'm tired or downhearted, thinking of a lifetime of hard work and so little to show for it, it often happens a voice calls 'Miss Gene-e-eva!' and there comes a child, flying down the street with her arms open, and she runs up and gives me a great hug, and then I think maybe my life hasn't been a failure after all . . ."

"Get in the car, darling," Geneva commanded. "I'll take care of the bag." She drove a little English sports car with a luggage rack in the rear. "You're not to worry about a thing. Are you comfortable? I won't be a minute." When the bag was in place she settled herself in the driver's seat and turned on the ignition, and at the last moment gave Faith's hand a squeeze and said, "There now!" and away they went. She maneuvered the car like a racing driver and it was always exhilarating.

So they left 6B behind again, the little fourth-floor world, and the drab city streets fled past them.

And Faith, rousing herself to the real world, asked, "Have you seen Anne?"

"Yes, I saw her Thursday." Besides her studio classes, Geneva taught at a number of private schools, including Anne's. "She asked after Mother, of course."

Faith flinched. When Geneva said *Mother* instead of *you*, another second-hand, chimeric figure rose up in dignity, kindred to the Two Fine People: the responsible mother-head, Anne's would-be mentor. "You didn't tell her I was in the hospital again?"

"No, certainly not. But she worries about you, you know that."

Faith made a silent groan.

"And Tony?"

"He's fine. We watch TV together at night, until I nod off. He means well, Faith, he really does, he's really very touching. He means to please, he's so considerate."

"Yes. Yes, he is." It was an old story: with other people —her mother, Geneva, their friends—he was so admirable, successful and debonair, and Faith seemed the defaulter. She couldn't explain it to anyone. She had asked Tony not to visit her any more at 6B. He had come one night when she was playing poker in the solarium with the other patients, and although she had broken off at once she had seen the repugnance in his eyes, his nostrils slightly distended. 6B was unseemly! He was terrified that she would introduce him, and she whisked him away. But in her room they had little to say to each other, and he kept looking at his watch . . .

The little English car swept into the drive and came to a halt. "You go inside, darling, I'll follow with your bag."

"Just let me carry the—"

"No, no, no. Leave everything to me. Go *in*."

But Faith didn't want to go in alone. The river roar hung in the air like a mist. The gray façade, the empty windows enclosed the desolation she had experienced there as if it had a consistency of its own and remained within intact. Anne was gone. Tony would not be home until late. The moment Faith stepped inside, she knew from experience, she also would become a ghost.

"I order you to leave that house!" Dr. Pomeroy had told her, more than once, still believing her primary problem was marital: "As your doctor I order you. If you have any trust in me you will obey my orders!" But her own fatalism, or masochism, her pity for Tony, or perhaps simply the dull, terminal inertness of spirit, the sense of disease, the not-caring any more, paralyzed her. She might have been acting out a preordained drama which she had to live through to the end.

Heedlessly Geneva flung open the door. Faith crossed the threshold and then turned around, speechless, in the hall, to watch Geneva bring in the bag. "So. There we go!" Geneva carried everything briskly up to Faith's room, and

Faith followed her, already silently crying, Don't leave me, don't leave me!

"Now, darling, I have to get back to town for my four o'clock class. Why don't you lie down and rest? Would you like a cup of tea? A glass of milk?"

"No. No, thank you. *Thank* you, Geneva, for bringing me home."

"Don't thank me. I wish I could do more." The soft hair and temple next to her own. "Will you be all right?"

Geneva's invincible goodness, her health of spirit seemed only to set Faith apart, undoing the consolation of 6B. It seemed to sever her tenuous hold on existence and to set her adrift. Where did she belong, where could she go? She was sinking, she couldn't help herself, she was sinking again. It was like a long scream beginning. There was even a sensuous satisfaction in giving way to it, in not resisting. Her eyes filled with tears.

Geneva cried, "Look, why don't you come with me? Come to class with me! You could try a few of the exercises —it would make you feel better, relax you. Or you can just watch, whatever you want. Just play it by heart. Oh, do come!"

She wanted to go with Geneva, she longed to lose herself once more in the warm golden tumult of the studio, but she knew she would feel more alone, sitting on the sidelines, more ill, than if she stayed here in the house. She shook her head.

"Oh, please come, Faith!"

I want to, I want to! "Thank you, Geneva. I'd love to, but I think I'd better not—"

"Just put on your coat again and come!"

"No. No. Hurry now, you'll be late."

She stood where Geneva had left her in her bedroom and listened to the sound of the departing car, the gutty snort of the exhaust as Geneva shifted gears. Then she went to the bathroom closet and took out the bottle: her real medicine. She had known all along she would do this.

The first gasping swallow eased her. The silence of the house was at once less menacing.

Carrying the plastic cup, she wandered down the hall to her studio, originally a north bedroom. She entered quietly, as if into a laboratory of living organisms, as if some evolutionary metamorphosis might have taken place there in her absence. But the room merely contained in its stasis a past self. The paintings, still stacked against the wall for the Georgetown show that had never come off, proclaimed a former painter. The painting on the easel, which she had left unfinished weeks, months ago, with its somber color, purples and blues, stabs of cerise and lime, laid on violently with a palette knife, told her that it, too, was her former herself, the former life of her life. Roughly she turned it about, its back to the room.

She perched on her high stool, nursing her cup, lacking the strength to turn the other paintings. They were an affront to her, a steady, incontestable accusation even more devastating than the sight of Anne's tight face. She told herself she couldn't be expected to paint when she felt so ill, was so often recovering from the displacement of 6B; but this death of her work produced a guilt which even the protective mechanism of her brain couldn't screen out. It was not objective, compartmental or perpendicular but horizontal, lying heavily at the base of her being, the ultimate self-betrayal, the ultimate loss.

She got up again, slowly scraping her feet under her and raising herself with an effort, rheumatically, turning her back on the pictures. She moved to the window and opened it. She had painted this view in all seasons, communed with it, dissected, abstracted it—the lines of the tall trees rising against the wide illuminated space of the river canyon.

It was spring now, and an afternoon thunderstorm was rapturously gathering. The trees, pointillated with buds, lifted delicate traceries to the plum-colored air, and a fragrance rose from the earth as if drawn out of it by the hushed vacuum preceding the storm, a fragrance composed of the earth's swelling and perishing work—bark, buds, rotting leaves, moist nests of violet and bloodroot, even slugs, all uncurling things, all mingled with the taint of approaching rain and darkening sweet air and the great river sigh, all gentle and welcoming.

The first drink, after a week's abstinence, was having its effect: that brief, magical flooding through her veins of relief. Did she escape her real self, she wondered, or find her real self? It was the same magical sensation she had first experienced so many years ago, the one that had rescued her from the loneliness of the war, and although it had become elusive in past years, she still sought to capture it: the visionary moment, the liberating moment, removing her from deprivations, fear, loss!

She leaned at the window, her chin in her hand, and she summoned up the picture of the Beechwood living room on Thanksgiving Day, illuminated with watery light like a Dutch painting, glowing with rich color, and everyone in it imprisoned forever and glorified.

But Grace and Severance had died last year within a few weeks of each other, inseparably, although in her own mind Faith had never allowed them to die; a girl in her, sixteen or seventeen, still clung to them, idolized them. Her mother still lived in her uncle's Florida house, cared for by the gentle servants who had looked after Grace and Severance. Faith had gone down for a brief visit this past winter. Her mother's age, her uncertainty put an end to whatever resentments Dr. Pomeroy had not helped her expunge. Only Jack Farrell remained undiminished, as fiery as ever, as active and inventive. But she was thankful their meetings were infrequent, for in the face of his attainments and self-command she felt her own decline too bleakly.

Thunder sounded for the first time, close at hand, a dull abrupt thump, and at this signal the girlhood gods vanished from her vision, to be replaced at once by the solitary figure of Janice Pemberton, Janice who had put a gun to her head alone in wartime London. She had come back to haunt Faith in recent months—she had never really left, in fact, the small, winsome figure in white fur jacket and white kid gloves, lurking unbidden at the fringes of her mind. And in her mind Faith always made her a little greeting, *Hello, Janice, how are you?* as if to comfort her. *You aren't alone, Janice, you are remembered.*

But today the figure, coming upon the announcement of the thunderclap, looked back at her cunningly, and frightened, she leaped up from the stool and made her way to the lavatory off the studio where she kept another bottle.

"My deliverance!" she said aloud, for after the first drink she usually began to talk to herself. "The layman's panacea!"

She groped her way back to the window. It was almost as dark as night. The thunderstorm was about to begin. The earth was smothered, saturated with blue-black air. At the last minute a wind rushed up, dispersing the reverent stillness, churning the delicate branches, and bits of blossom slanted downward, leaves rose from the ground like birds and fled away. There was a white explosion, and then with a sigh, a surging surrender, the deluge fell.

Downstairs a door slammed and Faith heard Tony, who must just have got home, call out, and she watched him burst out onto the terrace below and fling plastic covers over the upholstered chairs and dash inside again. He called her name again from the foot of the stairs, but she didn't answer. He would go now to his desk as he always did and forage among bills and dividends and checkbooks.

She tiptoed into the lavatory and again returned with her replenished cup to the window. It was cold suddenly and rain spattered through the screen. She reached for an old sweater she kept handy and sat on in the darkness and flashing light.

God, she thought, where are You? I am at the end, I have nowhere to go, I am alone, I have nothing.

God was now a very small light in her, a distant pinprick of cosmic intelligence which would not or could not act in her behalf, yet watched her, frowning, impassive, implacable. Since the New York trip she had taken to beseeching it with three monotonous syllables, *God help me*, at night, at odd moments during the day, the times when she forgot her own name or where she was going.

She sipped at her fresh drink. The phase of consoling visions had passed but she had to go on sipping doggedly, automatically, even though the foul familiar taste now sickened her. This was one of the unintelligible culminations: she drank when she no longer wanted to, when it no longer had any effect, good or bad. She had to. The question the guardian mechanism would not let her ask, let alone answer, was whether she could, or would, stop drinking if by some miracle Dr. Pomeroy could remove her depression. Someone had remarked recently—a remark so telling that she had blotted it away and couldn't even remember who had made it: "Not everyone who gets depressed has to drink."

All she knew, all she would let herself think, was that she couldn't stop *now*.

The door opened softly behind her, and turning, she saw Tony standing in the half-darkness. A wink of lightning showed his face to be apprehensive, pleading, lonely, too. Her heart went out to him.

She said softly, "Hi, dear."

"Faith." He crossed to her and put his arms around her. "Oh, Faith."

But she felt at once, Don't pinion me with your needs, your sorrows—don't trap me! He wanted to kiss her on the mouth and she pulled away. They had forgone sex months ago; it was a no man's land between them. The thought of it, of his cool flesh touching hers, was unbearable to her.

"I didn't know you were back," he said. "I called you—"

"It must have been the storm," she told him evasively. "I've been sitting here watching the storm."

"Don't you want the light on?" Without waiting for an answer he touched the switch and the overhead neon light struggled silently into life, flooding the room with an obliterating blue-whiteness. "I just got home in time. It was coming down in sheets. I hate to think what traffic will be like."

She might as well have been just back from the A&P, she thought, as 6B. He never asked, How are you? Do you feel better? He never noticed her drinking, he never saw her at all! He lived now among his own obsessions— his job, the difficult people on the job, traffic, investments, the weather.

And yet he still had moments of touching tenderness, which only added to the weight of her own guilt and self-loathing, and made her feel all the more stifled by him.

"Come down and have a drink with me now," he said. "*Please.*"

"He doesn't love me," she told Dr. Pomeroy. "He

only needs me." And Dr. Pomeroy nodded, unimpressed, his eyes vague. It was a line she had read somewhere. She spent a great deal of time with books by psychologists and philosophers, Fromm and Horney and Tillich, as well as Gibran, even the Psalms, underlining passages she thought applied to herself and might help her.

"Oh, Tony, you know what happens when we drink together. We always fight. I can't stand that, not tonight."

"I promise you," he implored her. "I promise you it won't happen!" And again, as with Geneva, she wanted to be persuaded, she longed for someone with a positive force to overcome her reluctance, her paralysis. "Please come!"

"All right, Tony." And she hated the feel of her face, downcast, lachrymose, falsely yielding. "All right."

"I'll just wash up," he said, "and join you."

She might have known. Nothing could be so simple as going straight downstairs together. From the beginning of their marriage he had been loath to sit cozily with her, companionably; it somehow endangered him. Cleanliness was another of his latter-day obsessions, or evasions. First he must have his ritual: a fifteen-minute sit on the john, a long brushing of teeth, a long wash, change of clothes, clean handkerchief, fresh cigarettes, continuous opening and shutting of drawers and doors . . . while she sat waiting for him in the gray living room, too lofty to heat properly, alone...

Panic set in. "Tony, don't stop to wash—just this once!"

But nothing, no crisis, no amount of urgency, could deter him. He was smiling his tiny evasive smile. "I'll only be a sec," he told her. "I'll be right down."

"Oh, never *mind* then." She was suddenly sobbing. "I'll get into bed. I don't want to come down anyway."

146

Then he was woebegone again. *"Please,* Faith. *Please."*

A grinding, groaning sound come from her throat. "Okay, okay, go ahead and wash." There was an unprecedented trembling behind her forehead, as if madness, the final coming-apart, approached at last, was upon her. "But hurry this time, don't be long, I can't stand sitting down there alone—"

"Yes, I'll hurry," he assured her, jubilantly moving off, oblivious of her tears, for they were not unusual any more. "I won't be a sec—" But she knew it would be forty-five minutes, as it always was. It had to be, lest he be threatened by his own private demons.

As she followed him out of the studio, her foot caught in the edge of a canvas and she gave it a vicious kick, denting it irreparably and scattering several other frames.

She sat leaning over her dressing table. After only a few hours away from 6B her face was heavy and dull again. What was the use of putting on fresh make-up? No amount of cosmetics could disguise the morose swelling, soften the glazed stare or remove the look of hopelessness.

Geneva came in as they sat watching the news before dinner, greeted them and went upstairs. When she came down she told them she was off to a master class; a distinguished dancer from New York was in town.

And it was Tony who cried, "Oh, please don't go, Geneva. Stay with us!"

And Faith echoed him: "Do you *have* to go, Geneva?"

Geneva hesitated only a moment, turning to them with a quick, grieving smile. How piteous they must have looked, the two fine people, afraid to be alone. She said, putting down her leather tote bag full of notes and books and odds and ends, "Of course. Of course I'll stay."

Faith must have lapsed into one of her blanks. They were all three on the sofa, watching TV. It was after dinner, and Geneva, who usually fell asleep, was rousing herself. Like most professionals with a trained body, she compensated for the demands on her by sleeping soundly. She said, "Oh my. I must get to bed. I have to be on my P's and Q's tomorrow." And she bade them good night and went upstairs.

Was there another lapse? Tony was rubbing her hand. The TV was still hoarsely talking. Faith said, "I must go up, too."

He didn't answer, leaning against her to fumble his tongue in her ear.

She wrenched her head away. "*No!*"

"Please," he said once more. "I have to." He was smiling, and she looked into his pinpointed eyes. The table of drinks scuffled away from the heave of his body as he flung himself on her. She twisted violently, the corded seam of the upholstery abrading her neck, and then somehow he had wrestled her to the floor and she had banged the back of her head explosively, and with one forearm crushing her throat, his shoulders and thighs nimbly, relentlessly, counteracting her struggles, his moist breath chuckling in her hair, he worked open his trousers. She seemed to see rather than feel the confused stabs and writhings of private flesh and the twinges of cloistered hair, the exploded back of her head, the crimson blood spreading warmly from her nose, the length of her whistling windpipe and the round of her stricken abdomen, and hovering over them like an insidious silent smile, the double fact of horror and pleasure. She surrendered suddenly, receiving him, and he rose over her, pinioning her wrists with his hands, and while his pin-pointed eyes insisted brightly on hers and his teeth grinned, he began to beat against her. And all the lamps around them softly glowed and the TV set barked indecipherably...

She found herself next in the lavatory of her studio, vomiting, rinsing the blood from her face; for some reason her nose was swollen. She opened the bottle and drank directly from it and at once retched up the liquor. Swaying, whispering, she clung to the washbasin; with one hand she held up her torn dress and slip, covering her blotched body. "Well," she said at last stuffily, her voice issuing from her clogged throat and nose as if she had been weeping. "Well, now."

She opened the lavatory door. She had locked the door from the studio into the hall, but she took care to move quietly, taking up the sharp knife which was part of her working equipment, grasping it, her fist vibrating. "Well, now." She ground her bile-gritty teeth. She turned the ugly painting on the easel around and tore it across with the knife.

Then systematically, weeping, grinning, she went from painting to painting, stabbing them, mutilating.

She unlocked the door and stole into the hall. The television set still muttered downstairs. She slipped into her bedroom and locked the door behind her. Geneva had left the light on for her in the bathroom, and she could dimly make out Geneva's form in the bed beside hers, flat on her back with her toes turned out, and hear her breathing musically like a little morning teakettle.

In the bathroom Faith poured out a tumbler of water and carried it back to her bedside. She sat down. Stealthily she opened the plastic containers—Seconal, tranquilizers,

Dexamyl, even the pills that relaxed the cramps in her hands and feet. And again carefully, systematically she began swallowing them, emptying each container and taking up another, rising to refill the water glass, returning, continuing.

It was like a consignment, a delivery. It wasn't even that she wanted to die. It was simply that she must put an end to herself, turn herself into something else, turn intolerable life, if need be, into non-life.

She lay down at last. She said, *God help me.*

8

It was a lighting fixture in a ceiling, a round radiant light in a porous ceiling. And then it was pain in her arms, which at length produced the question: What?

She looked to see.

Her arms were bandaged flat to boards and there were rubber tubes fixed with needles in the backs of her hands. And (*horror*) there was a tube in her nose, her throat. A small room, crowded with shining things, silver pipes and dials; something spelled OXYGEN. A vague murmuring, rustling, behind, above—people. A patch of strong sunlight lay splashed across a wall. The light in the ceiling looked down steadily at her: God?

Herself? Somewhere?

Her arms, aching, wanted to bend; she begged to bend them, whimpering. Someone mercifully freed her. The tube in her nose and throat was withdrawn, too, hand over hand.

The strong yellow sunlight slanted across the wall unalterably: *I am, I always am.* The bleak strong sunlight of childhood afternoons, all inevitable afternoons.

It was she, in this disgrace of metal and tubes, who was not.

She was in a cage. The sunlight was gone; night. A cocoa-colored nurse sat on the other side of the bars, sat perfectly still in a state of patience, not looking at her.

Faith couldn't sleep any more, twitching her feet and hands. The brown nurse turned and murmured gently, tried to make her more comfortable. The two of them, in the dead of night: the communion of comfort, of mercy.

She was in 6B again. But this was the little room with the window in the door, a room she had never been inside before, where only the very sick went, a man in DT's who howled all night, a woman in a tantrum . . . The shining pipes and dials had disappeared, but she lay in a bed with bars. She lay and looked, twitching.

The nurse had a black prayer book in the breast pocket of her uniform.

"Would you read to me, please, from your prayer book?"

"What would you like me to read?"

"The Twenty-third Psalm."

The nurse read without inflection. The words didn't have the desired effect. There was something false in this, the sad little scene in the timeless hospital-quiet of night, the humble colored nurse reading from the Bible to the privileged suicidal woman . . . "Yea though I walk through the valley of the shadow of death . . ." It was as if she had demanded, Make me cry, make a sad little scene, invoke the noble words, unbend me, open the floodgates, dissolve me, for I can pity myself when I shed tears, and God will pity me . . .

But the words didn't make her cry. The voice was too unemotional. The voice, the detached dignity of the nurse, the implacable ceiling light, condemned her. She lay in stiff, twitching, dry-eyed disgrace.

It was the nurse who shed tears at the end of the psalm, covertly, respectfully, only one or two, which she quickly dabbed away.

It was partly satisfying; someone had wept.

Morning. Dr. Pomeroy was talking to her with a wearied, cheerful forbearance, his voice coming from the same stern world as the sunlight: "Your respiration had all but stopped, your pulse was dropping . . . We reached a point where we couldn't do anything more for you . . ."

And suddenly she had an obscene picture of herself on a marble slab in the hospital morgue, herself marbled, her flesh drained: *gone.*

Dr. McAndrew, the general practitioner, friend and neighbor, who had been called in former crises, appeared too. Surprised, she chirped, "How did *you* know I was here?"

He answered shortly, "I *brought* you here."

They discussed her over her caged body. "It's her husband," Dr. Pomeroy said, explaining her, excusing her. "She wishes he were dead and she turns the guilt on herself." As simple as that?

Something false there, too.

Dr. Pomeroy, leaving, pressed her muslin-covered leg. But even he, after all, was removed now. The breezy, rather sexy warmth of former 6B interviews was lacking.

She lay after they left in a state of dissolution. She had abdicated their sunshine-world; she was debris. A few weak tears at last rolled out of her eyes into her temples, but her pity was a pretense too. They were tears for the person she had been, despairing, and was not now, debased.

Slowly her head rolled from side to side.

Nurses then, one after the other, morning-starched and lipsticked, began to come in to smile down at her, tossing her little bouquets of cheery words, and departed, as if she were on view. There was a caring-for-life, she realized, cowering, in the encouraging healthfulness they brought to bear on her.

Finally she asked for a mirror. "Oh, my God!" she cried, turning away from the yellow non-face framed in shards of dull hair. Somehow her mouth had got bruised and scabs blotched her lips.

"Well," they told her brightly, "you look a lot better than you did yesterday!"

She lay not thinking but sensate, permitting pieces of thought, or pictures, to come and go under the steady glare of the ceiling light.

She knew this at least: the suicidal death was obscene. She saw it, she looked it closely in the face. *Nothing.* Spent flesh on a marble slab, the face closed forever. A nothingness of passionless hate, its angry zero, its despairing naught, imprinted forever, lasting, extending forever in timeless time.

She knew this: there was nothing so irretrievable as the distance of death. (Anne, what would I have done to you? She had a picture of a young, solitary Anne, abandoned by a forever-death, consigned to a forever-goodbye.) There was no loneliness as inexhaustible. Nothing as comfortless.

She had come within a last breath of it. "... and your pulse was dropping . . ." The nurses were drawn to the room to look at her because she was a phenomenon. "We reached a point where we couldn't do anything more for you..."

The ceiling light continued to stare inexorably down at her like the eye of God.

Sternness encompassed her, waited upon her.

And in the stunned terror of this close look at death the last substance of resistance drained from her, pried loose from the wasted frame—stubbornness, denial, excuses, will—the substance of life before yesterday. She felt as if the essence of herself had indeed died, even the will to despair, as if it had been left behind in yesterday, and only her body, this shell, remained.

Or as if she had been reborn in embryo, a minute divested spirit in a withered organism, feebly waving a single tentacle of life.

Now then, the empirical Eye warned her.

But there was nothing left to reconstruct with, to say no with, or even, yet, yes.

Geneva was there, indomitable, colorful in this scene of pallor. But even Geneva belonged to yesterday.

"Don't tell Anne," Faith entreated. "Don't let Tony come."

It was Geneva who had called Dr. McAndrew. Setting off to one of her schools, about to step into her little car, she had hesitated, turned around, gone back into the house and up the stairs for a second look at Faith. "There was something about your breathing..."

Another miracle?

Blithely one day the attendants seized her, lifting her onto a stretcher cart, and the walls whirled around her as they sped her out of the little room and down the corridor and around the corner, and a moment or two later she was deposited in a brown semi-private room.

Another stage of purgatory, lower even than the resuscitation room with the window in the door: Hell was brown! "Can't I have a private room? I've always had a private room!" A last cry of self-distinction. But everyone smiled vaguely; they would see, they were pretty crowded right now...

Her roommate was a large silent woman who lay most of the time on her side with her rump turned to the world.

It was a hot night and the windows were opened wide. Faith lay awake all night, twitching, jerking, listening to her roommate's snores and the drunken laughter and orgasmic shouts from the derelict houses across the street from the hospital. Her eyes had begun to project shifting patterns on the walls of the room, like lantern slides, and when she closed her lids she saw the fronds of marshes, or sea anemones, blood-red, hysterically writhing. *Hypnogenic hallucinations*, Dr. Pomeroy had called them, for she had seen them after previous admissions, and she was thankful there was an abstruse name for them. But Dr. McAndrew had asked bluntly, "Faith, how much do you drink?" and she had answered, "Oh, a few highballs before dinner," and while he looked at her in baffled silence, she almost believed herself.

In the morning she was encouraged to get up. Stooped,

dazed, she staggered about the corridors, the floor heaving under her feet, and the world she had been brought back to, even the world of safety in 6B, appeared every hour more alien to her. What bodily strength remained seemed to be quivering away. She lay down, then restlessly got up to circle about, and then had to lie down again, mindlessly, like an animal in distress. Perhaps at this point the mortification of spirit, of the last vitality of brain and body, was complete.

She managed finally to make her way to the floor station, where she said in an extremity of appeal to a startled, upturned face, *"I feel so awful."*

She floundered back to her room. A few minutes later a house doctor arrived to look at her, and at once, without a word, administered a hypodermic.

Jeff stood in the doorway.

There were no surprises for her any more. In fact, there was nothing that was not strange within her and without, and she accepted now whatever happened dumbly, in total submission. Jeff's appearance was simply another manifestation of the unexplained forces controlling her. (Later Dr. Pomeroy explained. It was the law. One couldn't leave the hospital after a suicide attempt except in the custody of a member of the family. He wouldn't let her go with Tony, and her father was in Italy. He remembered then that she had a cousin.)

Jeff said, "Hello, Faith," and stepped into the room, but didn't advance further, preferring to lean against the wall there, his arms folded. He was smiling, not the smile with which the well derogate the illness of the unwell, concealing pity or discomfort, but one of paradoxically humorous seriousness, perhaps a trait of his changed self, neither kindly nor unkind, but obdurate, akin to the Eye, saying, *Now then.*

A momentary surge of shame flushed over her, for her desiccated unlovely self, her scabbed lips, her purple hemorrhaged hands where the needles had been inserted, the mudbrown room, the lump of her roommate. Had he come all the way from New York? She said, croaking, that it was good of him.

He didn't answer that. He asked quietly without preliminaries, "Faith, do you think you have a problem with alcohol?"

She felt an echo of the white explosion he had startled in her once before, now reduced to a faint pop of agitation, for even this shock was part of her inescapable state, target of the encompassing censure. And all contention, all defenses, had been so undermined, the protective shutters rendered so inoperable, herself so diminished, that only a denuded fact, lying virginal on the floor of her brain, revealed itself in answer: she could not stop drinking. This much she knew, at least.

"Yes," she answered, with a little rattle of the heart, "I guess I have."

A long time later she realized if the entire hospital staff—great-hearted Dr. Pomeroy, disapproving Dr. McAndrew, all the impersonal house doctors, all the friendly nurses—had gathered in one insuperable body to put this question to her, she might yet have answered no, if only automatically. But because it was Jeff, for whom she had always felt a compassion, almost a complicity, whose serious smile told her he could not be deceived, she could do no less than offer him the fragile truth.

158

When he asked her if she would try AA, she answered again, appalled, yes.

Without being fully aware of it, she delivered herself to his direction. Perhaps she had learned, staring at the Eye, the Eye staring at her, that she had surrendered the privilege of choice, that she had made an ending of herself and the beginning was not in her.

They were on their way to New York in Jeff's car.

She had not been allowed to go home even to pack a suitcase, but had made up a list of items which Geneva brought her. With Dr. Pomeroy's approval, Jeff was taking her to the New York hospital where he had received specialized treatment. "You'll like Dr. Fitzmaurice," Jeff told her. "He looks like a retired Shakespearian actor." He considered. "A retired Irish Shakespearian actor."

It was another move in the unfolding strangeness. She even had a feeling of holiday, at first, heading north with Jeff, away from 6B, away from the gray house. Geneva had told her Tony was in bed with a bad cold. What would have happened if she had gone home? Would she have taken up where she left off, turning helplessly to the bottle again? More than likely—if not at once, eventually. How else did she know how to endure life there?

But Jeff declined to dwell on her difficulties with Tony. "The only thing that can get me drunk," he said cryptically, "is alcohol." Persistently he talked about alcoholism, and her ears, her brain couldn't follow him. She stared straight ahead in stunned silence.

She was going to stop drinking, she was going to have to. She knew instinctively she could not go on living if she didn't stop, that there was some shrouded connection, for her, between drinking and dying. At the same time, she didn't know how she was going to live if she *did* stop.

Alcoholic! The dreadful word which Jeff used so freely had for her no less a demeaning, sordid reference than it had at the Montclair AA meeting, but now it had as well a sound of finality, crushingly dogmatic, eliminating for good all equivocation. Jeff himself had stated it was an incurable disease: "Once an alcoholic, always an alcoholic." She looked back into what already seemed another life, at the words "psychoneurotic depression," at Dr. Pomeroy's baffled but inexhaustible patience, at the voluptuous, genteel, romantic twilight of her years of desperation. To allow them to be explained as *alcoholism* seemed too simple, too paltry, too degrading an answer!

Should she go to Alcoholics Anonymous for six months and then drink again—prove to herself whether or not she really was an alcoholic?

As if reading her thoughts, Jeff said, "Try not to think of it as giving *up* alcohol, but as getting *rid* of it."

Yes. She sighed. Yes, she had to admit, it made sense. Her shoulders eased a little against the seat cushions. Yes, she would try.

They were bowling along the Jersey Turnpike. She began hesitantly to ask questions, which Jeff readily answered, throwing in ludicrous examples of the vagaries, conceits and self-deceptions of alcoholics: ". . . He wouldn't go to an AA meeting in his own home town for fear someone he knew might see him. Of course, quite often he had been seen passed out on his own front lawn on Sunday morning . . ." And she had to laugh.

How curious her laughter sounded—irresponsible, traitorous! But yes, again yes: she had entertained some of the same grossly ingenuous misapprehensions. It *was* funny, when you came to think of it, when you could laugh about it with someone else who understood it.

He said, "You see, if you want sobriety you have to be completely honest about your drinking..."

She sighed again. The word *sobriety* was as absolute, as abysmal as the word *alcoholic*. She was aware not only of being hastened into unknown territory, but of receiving the first fundamentals of an indoctrination, willy-nilly, of hearing the first essential words of a foreign language, a language in which even the jokes necessitated a foreign sense of humor.

And again she was impressed by Jeff's light-hearted seriousness, his easy, knowledgeable leadership. Why was he putting himself out so for her? They had never been on such a footing before. She could only accept, unquestioning. Perhaps their early, un-close cousinship had been a valid foundation for this crucial collaboration, the one leading and the other submissively following. Perhaps if they had been familiars, prone to favor one another, she might not have trusted him now so implicitly, with such awe.

In the Howard Johnson's where they stopped for lunch her body jerked in a violent spasm, and by the time they reached Manhattan she was hallucinating again.

Timorously she asked Jeff, "Do you see lights flashing on that billboard?"

"No," he said. He added, "We're almost at the hospital."

They conducted her to a room overlooking the East River, such an unexpectedly beautiful room, with its view, its soft draperies, its own bathroom, that tears of gratitude sprang to her eyes. Jeff said, "I'll have some paper and some colors sent up to you. You might like to do some sketching." She turned away. She felt washed with waves of kindness; the tears ran down her cheeks. He left her to the

161

nurses then, but in the doorway he told her, as a farewell, "Be good to yourself." No one had ever said this to her before.

She stood at the window with her back turned to the nurses, swallowing and gasping in whispers, mopping her face with her hands.

"Come on, dear," the nurses coaxed. "Get right into bed."

She lay at peace in this room, day after day, scarcely moving—a state of security and innocence like that of the newborn, her window opened wide to the warm spring sunlight.

She was on the fourth floor, and she looked out on a musical-comedy scene: a park, trees blossoming with yellow-green leaves, a tall wrought-iron fence, a police booth guarding the fence, and a parade of characters of all ages—pushing prams, walking dogs, roller-skating, often pausing to chat with the policeman, and in the background the Mayor's elegant white mansion with its flag flying. Beyond, the blue river sparkled in the sun. It was endlessly charming, endlessly engrossing. At dawn, in the city-hush, she heard an oriole sing.

Her ravaged body responded at once to Dr. Fitzmaurice's treatment. All day long nurses came and went from her room, replacing the bottles of colorless liquid that seeped into her veins (she wasn't even curious enough to ask what it was), bringing the array of health-building pills, giving her injections, taking blood samples, delivering the delectable meals she had ordered from a sophisticated menu and which she hungered for.

At night, usually very late, Dr. Fitzmaurice burst in, and heedless of time, stayed to expatiate restlessly on one or the other of his favorite topics, alcoholism and the Catholic Church, both of which obsessed and baffled him. He did indeed resemble a veteran tragedian, with his arresting profile and the wings of silver hair over his ears, his nervous pacing and his passionate, melodious soliloquies. He was one of the few specialists in the city in the field of alcoholism, and the hospital staff openly humored and adored him. (But when, Faith wondered, did he ever find time for his family?)

On his first visit he at once prescribed Seconal for her, diagnosing her hallucinations and spasms as withdrawal symptoms from barbiturates, but this nonetheless prompted a long midnight lecture on barbiturate addiction.

"You didn't know there was such a thing?" He threw up his hands. "The ignorance of all this merciless dosing!" He devoted some minutes to explaining addiction in technical terms, something to do with cell structure. "You're fortunate to have survived even the normal nights of it, combining alcohol and Seconal, let alone the overdoses. And would you have cared if you had known what you were doing? No, this is part of the disease, the not-caring, the *malaise* of the soul. Well, I wish I could keep you long enough to withdraw you—you can't cut out barbiturates suddenly, you know, once you're addicted, you must be tapered off. Mind you, you'll never really sober up until you get off the pills, too!"

They insisted it was a disease, this incongruous alcoholism—Jeff, Dr. Fitzmaurice, the AA pamphlets Jeff brought her. Even the American Medical Association had come to agree on this, although Dr. Fitzmaurice extravagantly accused the profession, where alcoholism was concerned, of blind unlearnedness. It was a disease, he said, of the mind and spirit as well as of the body.

"And how many valuable people have been lost to it," he lamented, pacing to and fro, "gifted people, traveling the whole route, including the suicide! When all the while the obvious symptoms were there, the clue to their madness, their progressive despondency, their bewildered self-destruction!"

Perhaps it was so, Faith mused, alone. But her own shame, her disgrace, wouldn't let her off so easily. Her own drinking was colored with the looming moralistic *wrong* of her upbringing, her mother not speaking to her, the guilt of those solitary moments on her bed. She still saw her drinking, however helpless, as an excess of self-indulgence. A "disease" was still too simple an answer.

One night when Dr. Fitzmaurice stepped out of the room to give some instructions to a nurse, she stole a look at the chart he had left on the end of her bed. Had he put down the damning word?

It said, under Diagnosis: Hypoglycemia.

Mona, in town for a few days with Shem, came to visit her. It was permissible to order lunch for her, and they ate at a little table in the open window. Faith felt so surprisingly at ease, even vivacious, that she told Mona the truth of her condition.

"Oh no, Faith, you're *not* an alcoholic," Mona said, shocked, as Pamela had done long ago. "You couldn't be! You never drank that much. You never made a spectacle of yourself. Maybe you did drink a lot, but of course you've been unhappy. You've never been happy with Tony, it's no wonder you drank. No, Faith, you're really not."

"But you don't *know*," Faith exclaimed, inexplicably shaken. "You don't know how much I drank!" Even Geneva didn't know. Certainly not Dr. Pomeroy. "And I couldn't stop! You don't have to be on skid row to be an alcoholic." She tried quoting Jeff. "Only a few of the country's millions of alcoholics are on skid row. The rest are housewives, executives, priests, lawyers—anybody. People like you and me."

But Mona shook her fair head. "You're just not the type," she insisted, smiling. Nothing would convince her.

Faith let it drop. Why was she angry, defensive? Only a little while ago she would have fastened thankfully on Mona's pronouncement. Now, for all her misgivings, it was not what she wanted to hear.

"Yes, they may tell you that," said Jeff, over the phone. "It's part of the general ignorance of the subject, the old stigma. You told yourself, didn't you? You drank because you were unhappy, because you had problems. Maybe it was so, at first. But this disease takes over: pretty soon we had problems and were unhappy because we drank."

But most of the time she lay quietly watching the park in a state of peaceful detachment—the absence of terror, the springlike innocence. The paper and coloring materials Jeff had sent were untouched; she had nothing to express of herself, she had nothing to prove in occupying herself. (The destruction of her paintings, which she only dimly remembered, seemed a fitting close to the destruction of a past life. She couldn't dwell on it.) She couldn't read even a detective novel for more than a few moments, and couldn't remember what she had read. Her powers of concentration seemed to have been demolished, too.

Only the literature Jeff had sent registered, and sometimes she sat in the open window with it, looking at The Twelve Steps presented at the beginning of each pamphlet.

165

They, too, had a dismaying, unconditional tone (1. We admitted we were powerless over alcohol and our lives had become unmanageable), with their declarations of taking inventory, making amends, relinquishing the will to "God as we understood Him." She could admit only that she was powerless over alcohol. The rest of the Steps seemed meant for people of sterner stuff, of substance and commitment. Perhaps she was still too much of an embryo.

"Be good to yourself," Jeff had said, but even then there had been a note of sternness. He had not meant, Indulge yourself. Certainly he could not have meant, Indulge the cringing brown-shadowed creature, with her compensatory arrogance, whom she had all but done to death. Something more dignified was expected of her, a greater kindness than she had yet shown anyone, let alone herself, something like the unqualified, undemanding kindness Jeff had shown her. She gazed at the park and silently tested the words, letting them float on her brain, or what was left of it—their admonishing forgiveness, their sovereign wisdom, their foreignness. And a dim distant benign prospect opened to her, ineffably appealing, in which goodness, inescapable goodness from which she could not except herself, prevailed.

God? she wondered. Is this God as I understand Him? Or love? She couldn't think, she had no powers of reasoning. She knew only that the forces, or force, that had rescued her, had brought her now to a sample of exquisite peace, yet still waited on her; had possibly made her this offering of peace in exchange for a greater effort on her part than any she had ever before made.

Dr. Fitzmaurice, coming in that night, stopped short. "Have you looked at yourself in a mirror lately?" He smiled for the first time. "There's been some improvement."

The bloat had gone, the flush had subsided; clarity had begun to shine in eyes and skin; someone, she realized nervously, was emerging.

Dr. Fitzmaurice had told her she might dress and go out for walks, but it had turned unseasonably hot, and strolling the gritty streets of the neighborhood, she felt suddenly in limbo again, belonging nowhere. Loneliness pierced her, and she returned gratefully to her womblike room.

Jeff telephoned. "I've got permission from Fitzmaurice for you to go to a Manhattan meeting tonight."

Oh God, she must begin, then. Was this really for her, the sanitized embracement of hearty, organized strangers? The atmosphere of meetings (*any* meetings—Rotary Club, Junior League, Alcoholics Anonymous), so wholesome, so naïve, so desolating. Could she really render herself up sincerely to that?

Jeff said, "Do you remember Sally Sperling from St. Anne's? She remembers you. She's one of us. I have to get back to Montclair, but I've arranged for her to meet you there."

She had to laugh. One of us! Even graduates of St. Anne's could be members of Alcoholics Anonymous! Each time she boggled, the rug was whimsically tweaked from under her. And again there was nothing to answer Jeff but yes.

It was Sally Sperling who had been voted Most Popular. An honor student, she was a small, highly organized girl, keeping her own counsel and declining to indulge in gossip or histrionics; but she had a droll sense of humor, shy, mischievous black eyes over a slow, dimpled smile, and a warmth that, coupled with discretion, drew everyone confidingly to her. (How had she ever come to be an alcoholic? Faith wondered.) They had never been rivals, the Most Popular and the girl with the Biggest Future, but by the very nature of their opposite tendencies, the one collected and the other bending to every wind, they had not been intimates.

Yet now, as the dimpled face under the flowered spring hat revealed itself, and the remembered voice—slow, slightly quivering with amusement (although deepened with age, or possibly alcohol)—greeted her, Faith felt a bond spring into first life between them, not necessarily of their common weakness, but of being refugees from that decorous life, the senior class of St. Anne's, the quiet stately girls of the Depression.

Then, as Sally took her by the arm, Faith saw in her face the light-hearted seriousness. It was a feature they all seemed to share, these AA people. It seemed not to be accidental, but something almost concrete, established, like a common aftereffect of their triumph over, or liberation from, the soul sickness. It was not naïve or desolating, it was reassuring and enviable. One gave one's self up to it trustingly even while asking, without expectation, how, *how* it was accomplished.

Chatting congenially in her deep, mirth-quavering voice, Sally guided Faith into the side entrance of the church and up the stone steps of the foyer. It was an immense Gothic building occupying half the block, with many halls and anterooms at the back for various functions. They turned into a spacious auditorium and at once they were in a throng of men and women, talking and laughing like well-dressed members of a wedding reception (what Tony would have called *"nice* people"), a much larger gathering than the suburban meeting Jeff had taken her to. But, as before, slogans in Gothic lettering flanked the stage.

168

Now she could read them: *Think, Easy Does It* and *First Things First*. ("They may strike you as pretty corny," Jeff had said, "but they come in handy in a pinch.") And the same banner hung from the podium, stating formidably: *But for the Grace of God ...*

Contrary to the superior feelings she had had at the suburban meeting, Faith found herself with a sinking sense of inferiority. She alone, in all of this animated assembly, was not light-hearted. Before, she had disdained to join them; now she was in despair that she would not be able to. The years of misery, of plodding to and from the red mansion on R Street, of mooning at the river with what she considered profound, omniscient thoughts, had lost their elegiac appeal. Here in this gathering of the easeful, the reconciled, they seemed merely sad, wasteful, childish and unspeakably mistaken. As before, no one stared at her, but when her anxious eyes met another's, she was smiled at with an immediate, straightforward message she could not decipher and which discouraged her the more. How was she to make her way, whatever the way was, into this intimate alien community? Perhaps the effort tacitly expected of her was too great, the makings not in her. Once more she was the brown-shadowed outcast; she was "different," defeated before the start.

They took their seats. "Try not to compare," Sally advised, as if like Jeff she knew one's doubts before one voiced them. "Everybody's story is different. It doesn't really matter how much we drank or when or how long, and all that. What matters is what it did to us. Relax and listen."

The lights were lowered, everyone subsided. As before, a chairman introduced the speaker. And presently a tall woman was standing alone at the podium, saying distinctly, as if they were honored lines from one of the Greek classics: "My name is Pauline, and I am an alcoholic."

169

Afterward Faith realized this half-hour completed the separation of her life into two parts. When she left the hall, under orders to be back at the hospital by nine-thirty, she wasn't the same person who had entered it.

The woman, Pauline, had so plainly been delivered of disgrace. It was this that riveted Faith's attention despite her shattered powers of concentration. Indeed, in Faith's eyes the woman seemed to manifest a positive radiance of deliverance, of freedom from shame. From the moment of Pauline's first utterance, "I am an alcoholic," declaring herself without pride or mortification, Faith hung on every word as she had once incredulously observed Jeff doing.

She might never have been to an AA meeting before. Perhaps the difference was in the speaker, this time an educated woman. Or was it perhaps in herself? After all, the woman from Passaic had exhibited in her own way the same radiance. But Faith at that meeting had been on the defensive, her guardian brain at work to protect her, screening out all that might apply to her and giving ear to all that she felt did not. Pauline worked in a Manhattan advertising agency, and the circumstances of her life and her drinking were for the most part as dissimilar to Faith's as those of the Passaic woman, but tonight a momentous underlying premise—the mounting terror, the growing helplessness—began to take form, so piercingly familiar to Faith that listening was like accompanying. She received every other sentence with a painful start of recognition—the repeated small explosions in the sensitive area where the years of guilt were stored.

Words loomed out of Pauline's story, as they had done on the Jersey Turnpike with Jeff.

Compulsion, Pauline said. "After the first drink, the first swallow, I didn't want to stop." Yes, yes. "Even while

I was drinking the first drink my mind was on the second."
Yes.

Progression, she said. And Faith looked all the way back to the beginning, to the solitary glasses of sherry here in the East Seventies, to the graduation, readily rationalized, from bottles to gallon jugs. No, all the way back to the first Thanksgiving Day drink, which hadn't been enough.

Blackouts: the strange amnesia?

And of course *disease,* the word Dr. Fitzmaurice sometimes hyphenated to dis-ease. And suddenly Faith remembered her anguished cry to Dr. Pomeroy, trying to tell him of the body-aching, brain-fouled, spirit-starved sickness . . .

"Science hasn't yet come up with an answer to the cause or causes of alcoholism," Pauline was saying. "And we in AA don't try to figure out why we drank, any more than a diabetic has to know why he has diabetes. Maybe we drank for confidence, or to fill a void, or to escape reality, but what difference does it make now? The important thing is to accept the fact that we have this disease today, that it's incurable, that no alcoholic has ever been able to return to normal drinking."

Ah, but how to live without it? How—forever?

"We don't pledge ourselves never to drink again. That would be an endurance contest, it would take will power, and an alcoholic has no will power over alcohol." She paused an instant, and then she said, "We stay sober on a daily basis, twenty-four hours at a time. Which we can break down to one hour at a time if necessary, or even ten minutes. We stay away from that first drink for one day."

One day! Instantly the life-long penalty shrank, the intolerable burden felt lighter. *Forever* vanished.

"We go outside ourselves, since we are powerless over alcohol, and ask a Power greater than ourselves to help us go one day without one drink, and if we are successful we thank Him at the end of the day."

God? It was a tall order after all.

"Any power of our own choosing," Pauline said. "The AA group, if you're an agnostic. I have a friend who prayed to the order of the universe, but after a while, for convenience' sake, he shortened it to God." A murmur of laughter. "Any power, so long as we don't try to rely on our own will. If we could rely on ourselves we wouldn't need to be here in the first place. If I were to decide to go it on my own again, without outside help, I could very easily forget what I am, and it would only be a matter of time before I convinced myself I could drink again, or I would use some emotional upset as an excuse. And for us this is a matter of life and death."

Yes. Yes.

"We attend meetings, many meetings, so that we won't forget, so that we can help each other. It's called sometimes the Disease of Loneliness, but together we're not alone. We have twelve suggested Steps which outline a way to live comfortably without alcohol and cope with the emotional upsets . . ."

But Faith's concentration had begun at last to flag. She could assimilate no more.

Pauline was finishing. "Yesterday is gone," she said, "and tomorrow isn't here yet. Today is all we have."

A burst of applause.

It was after nine. Faith thanked Sally, who promised to drop by the hospital the next day.

Spent, dazed, Faith rode back to the hospital in a taxi.

Yet she felt expanded, filled with a tentative wonder, an inkling not so much of hope as of possibility.

It was possible to be an alcoholic; it was possible for her to be one. It was possible to be one without disgrace. It was possible the disease was the answer, in Dr. Fitzmaurice's words, to her madness. It was possible Tony was not to blame for her drinking, or the shadows of her mother and father and the years in the Beechwood house. Plenty of people with unhappy lives did not take to drink.

There were no excuses left; there seemed to be no other answer. The tangle of her life had unwound to a single thread. It was an answer she had no choice but to accept.

She felt now not as if she were being led or driven into unknown territory but as if she had arrived in it, willy-nilly, dizzy and out of breath. And everything that had gone before in her life now lay outside, beyond the boundary she had crossed. She was not without trepidation. What was going to become of her? For certainly something was about to become, the reflection of a new face in the mirror told her that.

Would she be able to paint again, for instance, or would this new climate of essentials divest her of that too, sterilizing the intricate breeding ground of art?

But the tall woman had said Now, and in fact, Now was all Faith was capable of grasping. *First Things First,* one of the slogans had said. She wanted only to get back to her hospital bed. Maybe tomorrow Sally Sperling would explain the formidable Twelve Steps. Faith looked forward to telling Dr. Fitzmaurice, who had a somewhat parochial suspicion of AA, about the meeting. She wondered if she should stay in the hospital long enough to be withdrawn from the barbiturates. Why not? She was in no hurry to go anywhere. And Dr. Fitzmaurice had said she would never really sober up otherwise.

She was beginning to speak the language.

9

Two years had passed. Anne was graduating from Miss Mountfort's school.

Fanning themselves with commencement programs, the parents sat in a sloping amphitheater, only partially screened by towering trees from a hot June sky. A gentle clergyman offered the invocation. Behind the podium the graduating class was seated in a wide semicircle, ankles correctly crossed, daisies cradled in the left arm, faces pale and inscrutable. Faith wished Anne, near the middle of the row, would smile and do credit to her seventeen-year-old beauty, but the girl remained locked in solemnity like her classmates.

Faith and Geneva sat high up at the back of the amphitheater. Tony and his new wife were down in front. Faith could see the top of his polished, still-boyish head, and next to him Cynthia's premature gray. Even Dr. and

Mrs. Pomeroy were there, off to the right, for their daughter, too, was graduating. The difficult part would come later when they all must encounter each other around the refreshment tables, but Faith was more concerned about Geneva, who uttered little moans now and then and the burbling sounds of suppressed mirth. A decorous assemblage such as this and its contingent niceties, its dainty mishaps were apt to send Geneva into uncontrollable fits of laughter.

For herself, to her surprise, Faith was untroubled. She had expected the graduation to be an ordeal. It was nearly two years since she had set eyes on Tony and she had never met his wife, Cynthia. Even returning to Washington, scene of such trauma, was hard for her, and taking off from La Guardia she had steeled herself, said a little prayer. Now, unexpectedly, she felt forbearing, resilient, amused. Perhaps it was due to Geneva's burbling. Perhaps to the blue June sky and the graciously landscaped grounds which rolled away to the river; the out-of-doors always moderated things for her. A mockingbird atop a tall evergreen was running vigorously through its repertoire, all but drowning out the clergyman. Miss Mountfort, seated to the right of the podium, tweaked a quelling eyebrow, but the bird, even more imperious, shrieked on. Insects went sailing in precarious zigzags over the assembled heads.

An associate justice of the Supreme Court, uncle of one of the graduates, now rose to deliver the principal address.

Faith, as she so often did when lost for the moment in her new private world, looked up and about her and beamed. Genteel parents, intimidating headmistresses, former husbands, former psychiatrists lost their importance when matched against sky, bees, singing birds. Geneva's mirth was not ill-advised. In the midst of this function, so

175

weighted with self-satisfaction, some immense joke of life was revealed. Faith wasn't quite sure what it was. But the answer for her was always the same now: it was good to be alive.

Everyone was clapping. Faith joined in. Geneva touched her hand and said, "You have a new face." Faith lifted her brows in wonder; it wasn't the first time she had heard this but it still astonished her.

Then the diplomas were dealt out—Anne did smile, at last, a flash of relief—and finally everyone rose to join in prayer, and Faith thought: Take care of her, please, wherever she goes. Even if she doesn't believe in You, yet, please believe in her. How presumptuous! Constancy—and Faith told herself she should know this as well as anyone—was not something one needed to ask of God. Nor had she the right to ask that Anne be spared unhappiness. What then? But everyone was saying "Amen" and Faith said it too, a little late. So be it.

The ceremonies were over. The girl graduates came to life, crowing noisily. Parent turned to parent: Wasn't it charming? The niceties commenced. Geneva burbled. They made their way down the slope and into the throng.

Anne found them, hugged them. "Wasn't it delightful when the mockingbird out-invoked Dr. Forbes?" What a remarkable child, able to look so closed off when she chose and yet not miss a thing! And Faith thought: She is more mature than I am, she has always been; she has had to be. It wasn't a sad thought any more; it was something to be grateful for. Anne stepped back. "Oh, Mother! What a *mar*-velous costume!"

"It's not too wild?" She was wearing an expensive dress of orange and pink chiffon and a broad-brimmed straw hat trimmed with orange poppies. She was still not above dressing for courage. "I don't look too much like a lady poet—?"

"Oh no, it's *mar*-velous! No, you look like—like—an Irish countess!" They laughed, and Geneva's great Ha-ha-ha made people turn to smile.

Wendy, Anne's closest friend and classmate, joined them. "Hello-o-ohh, Mrs. Pemberton!" she breathed airily, touching Faith's cheek with her own, flinging her long arms and legs gracefully about. She lived in New York and during vacations was a frequent visitor to Faith's apartment off Lexington Avenue. "O-o-o-ohh, and Miss Gen-ee-va!"

Everyone was surging to and fro over the grass. "Come and have some punch, Mother, it's harmless. I'd better go and find Daddy. I won't be long."

But in their progress to the punch table Geneva, as was to be expected, was waylaid by parents and pupils, and Faith went off to pay her respects to Miss Mountfort, who obviously didn't recognize her. Miss Mountfort's eyes took in Faith's striking costume and suspected something inimical to authority. "I'm Anne Pemberton's mother," Faith told her. "Oh, how do you do," said Miss Mountfort, with a face like granite, and firmly she passed Faith along and greeted the next in line.

"Well, Faith, here you are." It was Dr. Pomeroy. "I've left my wife with a gaggle of graduates. I want a word with you." He took her by the arm and they strolled out of the thick of the crowd to the dappled shade of the trees. Faith had seen him once since leaving the hospital in New York, but that was a long time ago. She couldn't remember what they had said. Even when she had thought she was well, she realized now, she was still in fact convalescing.

He halted. "Let me look at you." He was a little grayer at the temples, but his face was as interested, as audacious as ever. He said, "You are quite the most glamorous thing at the party." She colored; he had never shirked a compliment. "Faith, are you still—?"

"Yes, I'm still." He meant, of course, still not drinking.

"It's been over two years now, hasn't it?"

"Yes. But only one day at a time."

"Let's sit down a minute." They had come to a rustic bench. "You are very desirable. I hope you have a lover."

Her color deepened; he took a very dim view of the celibate life. "No, I haven't. I expect I will someday. I have a couple of beaus, but nothing terribly serious. It's enough of a job getting myself together, becoming someone— being born." How extraordinary and delightful to talk of lovers and rebirth under the trees, while the hubbub continued in the offing and family groups attractively formed and re-formed before them.

"You're not carrying a torch for Tony, are you?"

"No. I assure you, no. The divorce was painful, I don't deny that. I see now that it was more my failure than his, but once it was over, I stopped belaboring myself."

"I always felt when you solved that problem you would stop drinking."

"We had the cart before the horse. I couldn't have solved *any* problem if I hadn't stopped drinking first."

"Well, you sure as hell fooled me. I just had no idea you were drinking that much."

"Of course you didn't. Nobody did. I hardly did myself. I put a great deal of effort into fooling people, myself included." She turned to him. "But I will be forever beholden to you. Not only for keeping me alive, but for all the help you gave me—the enlightenment, which I can use now as I couldn't then."

"I'm glad." He had never really accepted gratitude. "What about your painting?"

"Oh yes, at last it's going well again."

He was silent an instant. He smiled and shook his head. "It isn't often that one sees a person resurrected." It was proof of his magnanimity: his genuine pleasure in her well-being, wherever she had found it. He gave her knee a final pat, as he had done at the end of his visits to 6B "Faith, you've got it made!" And he rose.

"Oh no," she exclaimed, rising also. "Far from it." She glanced at him anxiously, as if she couldn't for her own sake let him believe this. They were strolling back toward the refreshment tables. "Everything does not automatically come up roses. We don't expect it to." They halted again on the edge of the shade. "But we learn a kind of reconciliation—with life as it is, with ourselves. The ragtags, the good and the bad, get sorted out. And out of that terrible chaos we find simplicity. Or we try to, we begin to."

" 'We,' Faith?"

She grinned. "We, the resurrected."

He grinned, too, nodding. There was no more to be said. She gave him her hand in parting. But he bent and kissed her cheek.

She found Geneva chatting with Tony and his wife. Still flushed from Dr. Pomeroy's kiss, she greeted them. "Hello, Tony. Hello, Cynthia."

She had meant to spare Tony the embarrassment of introducing the new wife to the old, but his eyes chilled in a familiar disapproving expression. Cynthia, a little flustered, shook hands with inadvertent enthusiasm. Tall and athletic-looking, quite handsome and obviously well-meaning, she was one of those gangling well-bred girls Tony had always admired. Anne stood by, watching with a detached, large-eyed commiseration. And Faith was glad she had worn the outlandish pink and orange costume.

Geneva cried helpfully, "We've discovered Cynthia was an old pupil of mine!"

"That's not surprising." Faith smiled at Cynthia. She was determined in spite of Tony's distaste to vanquish all animosity. "It seems as if everybody was a pupil of Geneva's at some time or other."

"Yes, doesn't it?" Cynthia laughed. "And now my daughter." She had children by a former marriage. Tony was clearing his throat, a signal that he wished to leave.

Faith said, "You're looking well, Tony."

He cast a nervous glare at the refreshment table and said "Yes" shortly. Yes, Faith thought, commiserating also, what a pity you ever got mixed up with the likes of me: painters, dancers! How incongruous it seemed, now. But Cynthia was staring at him hopefully, and he made an effort. "*You're* looking well, too, Faith." And his gaze shifted to the crowd just beyond her shoulder.

"Thank you. It was a lovely commencement, wasn't it?" She didn't dare look at Geneva, who was beginning to burble softly again.

"Very nice. Well, Cynthia, I think we'd better move along. Goodbye, Anne, we'll look forward to seeing you in Nantucket."

"Goodbye, Daddy." Anne reached up to kiss him fondly. "Goodbye, Cynthia."

"Goodbye, goodbye." Everyone said it, indiscriminately, to everyone else, without shaking hands. Tony and Cynthia moved away. Geneva turned to the trees and erupted with laughter.

"Mummy, I'm going back to my room to change. Let's get out of here."

"Yes, let's." Faith was a little gaspy with laughter too.

She touched Geneva's arm. "Pull yourself together, darling, it's time to get us to the airport."

"I'll meet you at the car," said Anne, and vanished.

The gathering was breaking up. All around them the well-dressed people were kissing, shaking hands, proffering farewells. For a moment, waiting for Geneva to disentangle herself from yet another group of patrons, Faith took in the scene, the color, the affectionate voices, the sunlight and heavy green shade, the lawns undulating away into the shimmering distance, all so cultivated and so redolent, to Faith, of a past significance. And suddenly she felt disembodied, with something of the old feeling of not belonging, of being between two worlds.

But she would never come here again. The irreverent laughter still echoed within her. "My name is Faith," she said to herself, "and I am an alcoholic." It was this statement that gave her both the responsibility and the liberty to be what she was. It was always like this when she said it: amazement seized her, and a kind of comprehensive perception rushed cinematically through her mind, sweeping her from this graduation day and its Amens to the fact of her life, the fact not only of being alive at all but of living in thankfulness and freedom. If there were to be other milestones in her life, even other miracles, they could not be as great as this. It made her smile with the beaming springlike look, the face Geneva said was new. It made her eyes smart.

She turned and walked on.

Mrs. Crowe,
born in Manhattan,
lives in a one-hundred-fifty-year-old farmhouse
in New Hampshire.
She has published previous novels,
including *Northwater* and *The Tower of Kilraven*,
as well as many short novels and short stories.